saving sailor

a novel

renee riva

COOK COMMUNICATIONS MINISTRIES
Colorado Springs, Colorado • Paris, Ontario
KINGSWAY COMMUNICATIONS LTD
Eastbourne, England

RiverOak® is an imprint of
Cook Communications Ministries, Colorado Springs, CO 80918
Cook Communications, Paris, Ontario
Kingsway Communications, Eastbourne, England

SAVING SAILOR

Published in association with the literary agency of Alive Communications, 7680 Goddard St., Ste. 200, Colorado Springs, CO 80920.

Cover Design: BMB Design, Inc.
Cover Photo: Photodisc
Interior Design: Susan Rae Vannaman

First printing, 2007
Printed in the United States of America

1 2 3 4 5 6 7 8 9 10 11 12

ISBN 978-1-58919-091-7
LCCN 2007921089

I dedicate this book to my sibs,
who insist to this day
that Mom and Dad won me
in a bingo game.
Just thought you'd like to know,
it wasn't bingo, you idiots, it was bocce ball.

Acknowledgments

My thanks to all of you wonderful people who have contributed to my life as a writer:

Elaine, Dee, Lonnie, Myla, Kate, Diane, Glenda, Kris, and Gail.

Dorie, my childhood inspiration, where it all began on the merry-go-round.

My therapists: JoAnn, Celiene, Linda, Mike, Cris, and Dr. Leo Marvin.

Karen Harter and Alice Crider, my online comedy relief team for all the times I needed a good distraction. Thanks for always being "out there" for me.

Chip MacGregor, for my beginnings. Beth Jusino, for keeping me in print, smiling, and on caffeine. Jeff Dunn, for rescuing *Saving Sailor* from the slush pile and bringing it to life. And Jon Woodhams, for covering my tracks. Nick Harrison, for your encouraging words "send it out." Gary, my husband, for pursuing my dreams above your own, listening to my endless stories—over and over—and still letting me write above all else. My girls: Anna, Taylor, and Oksana, for tolerating 365 Happy Meals too many, and still liking them better than my cooking. You're the best.

To everyone who never thought it would happen, neener-neener!

I could not have written this book without my big, amazing Italian family; Leslie, Grant, Blake, and Gregg, who gave me a lifetime of material and taught me the true joys of sibling rivalry. We took it to a whole new level, didn't we, guys? Thank you, Mom, for putting up with us, and when necessary, washing our mouths out with soap.

In memory of my dad, Santo Benjamin, who taught us all to love much, live well, and laugh our crazy heads off. You gave us the best in life and taught us never to settle for less. How I wish you were here, but I know where you are. Save me a good seat on your left at the wedding feast in heaven. Mom already called dibs on your right.

Thank You, God. Thank You for our lives, thank You for The Life, thank You for The Truth, and thank You for The Way.

Introduction

When I was growing up, I thought I came from the weirdest family on earth. Now, as I look back on my childhood, I know I did. When I compare my family in those days with families of today, I see just how weird we really were. For one thing, there were seven of us, almost unheard of nowadays. For another, I had only one set of parents, and they actually loved each other. A lot. Scary, isn't it? And here's the real clincher—I had a great childhood. The kind where your mom stayed home and baked cookies for you and your family stayed in a summer cabin all summer and swam and water-skied and had candy night every Friday night.

What can I say?

Pretty much, just, *Thank God.*

Did I mention we weren't perfect? Well, we weren't. But perfect isn't what makes a great childhood. What makes a childhood great is being able to look back and remember the good over the bad, the laughter over the tears, and the love that covered a multitude of sins.

It's looking back to that one summer that stands out above the rest. You know … the one where you knew what really mattered in life: God, your dog, your hamster, and your family. Most definitely in that order.

Prologue

Many times there comes into our life a crosswind, a change in course that changes us forever. Often we don't know until years later just how much influence that event had on who we have become.

For some of us, it comes at a very young age; for others, late in life. For me, it came in the summer of 1968, when I was ten years old. It swept over me like an east wind when I was heading south. I can only describe it as an epiphany, an awakening in my young soul that told me there was something more to life than what I could see with my eyes.

Along with that awakening came the people and relationships that would determine how much or how little I would settle for in life, how far I would seek to find Truth. And true love. And the revelation that life is a wonderful gift of grace.

I look back on that summer often, when life feels more complicated than it should. The memories are never far from my heart and mind. I have only to close my eyes to see the water … cool, clear blue water. And when I breathe, I smell the sweet, warm summer air of my childhood.…

Drifting

Indian Lake, Idaho
July 1968

I'm sittin' in a rowboat in the middle of Indian Lake with my dog, Sailor. He's a collie-shepherd mix with one brown eye and one that looks like a marble. He's wearin' a bright orange life jacket, as any seaworthy dog should when playing shipmate. Sometimes we pretend we're on the high seas awaitin' capture from handsome rogue pirates. But today, we're just driftin'.

The oars lay on the floorboard of the wood dinghy; a slight breeze sweeps over us, rufflin' up Sailor's long fur. We're just soakin' up the sun and floatin' by the island where our family spends our summers.

My mama is reclinin' on the dock in her new Hollywood sunglasses. She's got a paperback novel in one hand and a glass of iced tea in the other. My big sister, Adriana, is slathering on baby oil, singin' along to her transistor radio. My big brother, J. R., short for Sonny Jr., is gutting a fish over on the big rocks, while the younger twins, Benji and Dino, are still tryin' to catch their first fish of the day.

All this is going on, while at the same time I'm in the middle of a conversation with God:

"... And so, Lord, if we get to pick what age we'll be in heaven, I choose nine years old, because I am havin' the best year of my life. I know I say that every year, but this time I mean it. And next year, if I change my mind, don't believe me. I promise it will always be nine."

I have this feelin' deep down inside that I will never change my mind. I just don't see how it can get any better than driftin' with my dog on a sunny afternoon, goin' wherever the wind takes us....

1

Indian Island

"A. J., you float your little fanny right back to this dock."

"Comin', Mama," I yell across the water. I think we have a family matter we're about to deal with here. Our family tends to have a lot of family matters. If you ask me, it comes from havin' too much family history. There are times I just want to say, "Ix-nay the istory-hay." Nix the history.

For starters: We are a Roman Catholic Italian family, and none of us are allowed to forget that. Anyone who puts that identification in jeopardy is dealt with severely. I was nearly disowned for trying to change my name to Dorothy Jones at school.

To make matters worse, there are two rumors I've had to live with my entire life. One is false. The other true. Contrary to what my sister has told everyone since the day I was born, my parents did not win me in a Mississippi bingo hall when I was a baby. And yes, my real name is Angelina Juliana Degulio.

I am a living legacy of two grandmothers who insist on preserving our *rich Italian heritage.* My name was settled in a coin toss. The dispute was over whose name would be first. Grandma Angelina won, but was accused of cheatin' by Grandma Juliana. They fight about it to this day.

The name Angelina, I am often reminded, means "angel," and I am the lucky child who gets to bear it. So, whenever someone asks me my name, I say, "Just call me A. J."

I'm workin' my way back to the dock, paddlin' with my arms over the bow of the boat. Once I'm in drift mode, I like to stay there. "Still comin', Mama …"

The one thing I've gotten away with up to this very moment has been my self-imposed Southern accent. My mama is just beside herself right now from hearin' me yell, "I'm floatin' down yonder, Mama." I'm the only one of her kids to call her Mama instead of Mom or use words like *y'all* and *yonder.* I don't do it to make her mad. I just picked it up from those old Western movies I watch. I'm still tryin' to figure out why they call them Westerns when everybody's talkin' Southern.

I think Southern is a beautiful language. I'm almost fluent now, but I have to watch it around Mama. Tends to get on her nerves. The closer I get to the dock, the more sure I am that "down yonder" must've really hit a nerve. You always know when you've gone too far with Mama.

You can see the blood rise in her face like a thermometer on a hot day. And it just keeps risin' 'til her true Italian temper kicks in. Like right now ...

"Angelina Juliana Degulio ..."

That's the next clue—she yells the whole embarrassing name.

"No full-blooded *Roman Catholic Italian* child raised in the Northwest can possibly have a Southern accent. You stop that Southern garble right now before I march you into the confessional at St. Peter's, where you can tell Father Sharpiro how you're dishonoring your family." That's my mama's way of sayin', if I want to stay out here on the water, I'd better zip it with the Southern lingo. If there's one thing I've learned about Mama, she plays life by her rules. You either follow them or you're out of the game.

Her name is Sophia, and she would like everyone to believe that she is *The* Sophia Loren from Hollywood. When she does herself all up, she comes pretty close. She has those same dark Italian eyes and adds that little swoosh of eyeliner. She even makes a point of getting her hair styled exactly like the actress's.

Mama's favorite game is to fool people into thinkin' she is Miss Loren. She can only go so long before she decides she just has to play this game or she will go nuts. If there's one thing Mama cannot tolerate, it's boredism. We'll all be layin' around the dock readin' or fishin', when suddenly, out of the blue we'll hear, "Miss Loren is goin' to town." Then she hauls us all off the island to go to town with her. We usually go somewhere real crowded, like downtown Squawkomish.

First off, we hit the corner across from the local hangout, Big Daddy Burger. Mama puts on her dark sunglasses, dabs on her Poppy Pink lipstick, and hands me a notepad and pen. "A. J.," she'll say, "after I get over there by that crowd, you all come running up to me holding out that notepad, yelling, 'Sophia, Sophia, can we have your autograph?'"

Adriana is so embarrassed she pretends she doesn't know us, but my brothers love this as much as I do. And, boy, do people fall for it. The next thing you know, everyone is swarmin' around my mama. Folks are pullin' anything they can out of their purses and pockets, even old gum wrappers, to get that autograph. The best part is, Mama says it's not even a sin because when people ask for her autograph she only signs her first name. She also says, "It serves these people right for being so gullible as to think that the real Sophia Loren would be spendin' her time at Big Daddy Burger, in downtown Squawkomish."

After she's done gettin' everybody riled up, we all pile into our turquoise Thunderbird convertible and laugh all the way to The Spaghetti House. Everyone, that is, but Adriana. I guess you can't expect a sixteen-year-old Prom Queen to think that's funny.

I'm watchin' Adriana right now from my boat. I can't believe how much time she spends just tryin' to get tan. That is really all she does all day—just lays there on that dock, with her iodine-tinted baby oil. It really makes no sense to me. She was born with a tan, for Pete's sake. She is already so dark, if you put a red dot on her forehead people would think she's from India.

Sometimes when I look at her, I wish I had dark hair and eyes like she does. I'm the only blondie in the bunch. People talk about Adriana with words like *beautiful* or *striking*. I only hear words like *cute* or names like *Freckles* when people talk about me. I also have this gap between my two big front teeth that makes me look like the guy on the front of *Mad* magazine. Mama says, "Who wants a white picket fence for a smile anyway?" The only good thing I can say about it is, I can squirt water between my front teeth farther than anyone I know, which comes in handy when you're livin' on a lake all summer.

I float past the dock pretendin' to be a fountain statue, squirtin' a stream of water straight up in the air. That really grosses out Adriana, which makes it even more fun.

"Take your big fat beaver teeth and go build yourself a dam," she yells.

My sister loves to torment me about my bingo hall beginnings and says that's why I look and talk different from the rest of the family. "What more could we expect out of a Mississippi bingo hall, than a sappy little towhead with a Southern drawl?" She also points out my taste in music: "While everyone else is groovin' to the Beatles, there you are wallowing in 'Moon River.'"

Sometimes, when I feel different from the rest of the family, I think of "Wolf Boy." It's a story I read about this little boy who got lost in the woods and was adopted and raised by a pack of wolves. When his family found him again, he acted more like his wolf family than his real family. I may be different, but I don't think I'm *that* different.

To tell the truth, I wouldn't want to be like Adriana anyway. I would rather be out here floatin' with my dog, not worryin' about what color I'm turnin'. I get tired of watchin' Miss Perfect on the dock. I toss a stick for Sailor, and he jumps right outta the boat and swims after it. Adriana gives me a look like I am just so immature to be playing fetch with "that big dumb dog."

"Hey, Adriana," I yell, "can't you think of anything better to do than waste your whole day layin' in one place for a stupid tan?" Then I remind her that true beauty is more than skin deep and maybe she should spend more time workin' on the inside.

She just yawns like it is hardly worth her time to respond, then says, "Oh, A. J., why don't you go join a convent or something?"

I smile when Sailor gets out of the water and shakes all over her. Wouldn't surprise me if they could hear her screamin' clear on the mainland. I load Sailor back into the boat. "Good dog," I whisper.

It doesn't bother me what Adriana thinks of my music, or anything else I happen to like. I am what Daddy calls "a hopeful romantic." I watch all those Westerns with The Duke and just melt over the steamy love scenes where he's kissin' his girl.

Daddy tells me not to settle for anything less in a man than what I see right there on that TV screen. "You get yourself a man's man, A. J. There's a world full of wimps out there who will put on a pair of cowboy boots and call themselves a cowboy. You just make sure you find the one who can actually ride a horse."

I have never told anyone this, but, I have got the biggest crush on Little Joe Cartwright, from *Bonanza*. I love to daydream about him. That's one of my favorite things to do when I'm out here in my boat. I just close my eyes while I'm driftin' along, and the next thing I know … I'm his girl. He's comin' in from a long day of wrestlin' cows out on the Ponderosa, and I'm cookin' up some dead deer stew for him. He comes into my big ranch kitchen and says, "Boy, that sure smells good," with that romantic Southern accent of his. Then he comes over and gives me this big ol' kiss. We kiss so long, the stew just burns away on the stove, and we have to have peanut butter sandwiches instead.

Now, he may not be as big and burly as The Duke, but he is cute, cute, cute. That goes a long way in my book. Besides that, he can ride a horse.

Right in the middle of my daydream, I hear the sound of our boat engine and open my eyes. My daddy must've gotten off work early today, because he's pullin' up to the dock, and it's not even four o'clock yet.

"Everybody in," he yells. "We're going for a ride."

I hear Adriana moan. She does not enjoy these family outings one bit. But Daddy had a talk with her last night about how we are a family, and like it or not, she needs to try and be a part of it. Then he told her how one day she will look back and miss these days, to which she rolled her eyes.

My daddy's name is Sonny. He's the park ranger at Indian Lake State Park on the main shore. We get to stay out here from the time school lets out in June, 'til it starts up again in September.

Daddy likes to call me Ficuccia. He was fed up with all the rivalry caused in choosin' my name, so he just came up with a name of his own. *Ficuccio* means "little fig" in Italian. Ficuccia would be a little girl fig, which is much easier to live up to than an "angel."

Daddy's a big man with thick black wavy hair and deep blue eyes. When he's pullin' away from the dock, a ray of sunlight hits his eyes. They look just like two blue jewels shinin' back at me. "Daddy, what did the girls think of you when you were young?" I ask him.

He glances over at Mama, then says, "I was a knockout in high school. Your mother had to fight all the girls off of me just to get me to notice her." Daddy gives Mama a big grin and starts to laugh.

"Sonny Degulio, that's a bunch of hogwash and you know it. There were so many boys swarming around me, I couldn't see through 'em all to have even noticed you were alive." Then she adds, "You wouldn't have had a chance if my mother hadn't forced me to marry you. You were her only ticket to Roman Catholic Italian grandbabies."

Daddy smiles at Mama. "Admit it, baby. I was hot. The Italian Stallion, remember?"

Mama just rolls her eyes, but she's smilin' too. I think Daddy won Mama because he can make her laugh. Nobody can make Mama laugh the way Daddy can.

A lot of folks out here own their own cabins and boats, but we are renters all the way. My daddy says, "Why would I want to buy a boat when I can rent the *African Queen* every summer?"

When a boat full of girls go by, J. R. yells, "Duck down," to my little brothers. "We look like a boatload of sissies."

We are the only family I know on this lake with a pink boat. But Daddy says this was just like the boat they used in a famous movie, *The African Queen*, and we should sit up tall and proud when we pass other boats. "They only laugh because they're jealous."

So Mama says, "Well, Sonny, since you're feeling so high and mighty in your pink boat today, let's see how tall and proud you look when this big fancy yacht up ahead passes by."

Daddy looks at Mama real sly, then grabs his ranger hat. He jumps on the bow of the boat and pulls his ranger pants up to nearly his chest. Now his ankles are stickin' out with his bright green socks. He's just standin' out there with his face to the wind in his ranger hat, lookin' ridiculous. He's stickin' out his chest and holdin' his pants up by his thumbs, just waitin' for that yacht to pass by us. We are all howlin' so bad, we can't even hide our heads.

So here comes the yacht right close to our boat, and people are lookin' at us like we are from Mars, and Daddy yells, "Afternoon, gentlemen. I know what y'all are thinkin', but there is no way we will trade our *African Queen* for your yacht, so don't even think about it."

Now Mama's laughin' so hard she just rolls right off her boat cushion onto the floor. That just makes us laugh harder. But Mama can't stop, and she sure as anything can't get up off the floor. So Daddy hops down off the bow to help her up, but she can't even take his hand. Then Daddy asks, "What's so funny, darlin'?" with an accent just like mine.

Mama can hardly talk, but she squeaks out, "Do you know who that was?"

Daddy says, "No, Soph, I don't. Why don't you tell me?"

So, Mama squeals, "Dr. Starky ..." and she's laughin' so hard now she's cryin'.

The reason that might seem so funny to Mama is because Dr. Starky already thinks we're a pretty nutty family, even before Daddy yelled from the bow in his high-waters. See, we've only been here for one month, and we've been to Dr. Starky's three times. The first time was when Benji got a fishin' hook caught in his bare back when Dino was casting. He was screamin' like a banshee. We couldn't pull it out without tearin' up his back, so we just cut the line and walked him into Dr. Starky's office with a fishhook stickin' outta his back.

Then on the Fourth of July, J. R. shot off a bottle rocket that went haywire and singed off part of his eyebrow. He was lucky he didn't lose his eye, but that put the kibosh on our Fourth of July. So once more we visited Dr. Starky with a weird injury.

Then, just last week, Dino had the great idea of pretendin' the island was his own private jungle, and Benji was the intruder who needed to be trapped and tortured. Once Benji stepped into his lasso, Dino pulled it tight around his ankle and dragged his captured prey back to base camp for Chinese water torture. Unfortunately, along the way, he was dragged through a beehive, at which point Dino dropped the rope and ran for it, leavin' Benji to fend for himself. Benji came screamin' through the woods, followed by a swarm of bees and his rope in tow. By the time he reached the cabin, he had so many bee stings Mama just threw him in the tub and soaked him in baking soda and meat tenderizer. A few hours later his whole face started to swell. When he walked into Dr. Starky's office, Benji looked like somethin' from *My Favorite Martian.* By the time Mama stopped laughin' at him, Dr. Starky was lookin' at her like she was just the worst mother in the whole world to laugh at her son like that.

What Dr. Starky doesn't understand about our mama is, when she starts to laugh about somethin' you really aren't supposed to laugh about, tryin' to stop only makes it worse. She said she's been that way since she was a kid, and has gotten in a lot of trouble for laughin' in school, church and libraries, even at funerals. Daddy's gotten pretty good about walkin' her out of those situations once it starts, because when she gets to laughin' like that, she's too weak to get up and run out herself.

After Mama recovers from seeing Dr. Starky on the yacht, she says, "Well, Sonny, if that man didn't already have enough doubts about this family, you just clinched the deal for us." She tells Daddy that the best part is yet to come because Daddy has to go to his office to get his mandatory tetanus shot for work next week.

Daddy says, "Well, maybe I'll just wear my Smokey Bear outfit for the occasion."

2

Backstage Actress
Act 1: Scene 1

None of us have any idea where Daddy is takin' us, but he had us girls throw on our sundresses before we left, so it must be someplace pretty fancy. Once we reach Jasper's Cove, he pulls our boat up to the dock right outside of Smitty's Tackle Shop. "Fishin'? We're goin' *fishin'?*" I ask.

"Nope. Everybody out," he yells.

We all end up on this dock down at the end of the lake, surrounded by Western shops that look a hundred years old. You kind of expect The Duke to come walkin' down the street and lay a "howdy" on ya.

"This way," Daddy says, and we all fall in line behind him. Mama pulls out her Hollywood sunglasses, and I'm thinkin', *Not here, Mama, oh please, not now.*

She just looks around like she's not sure what we're in

for either. Then Daddy takes us all across the street to this big wooden building that has a reader board on it:

NOW PLAYING: ANNIE GET YOUR GUN

"A play," I yell. "This is a playhouse, and we're goin' to a play."

Adriana gives me a look. I can't help it. We have never been to a real playhouse before.

"It's not only a play," Daddy says, "it's a dinner theater." He smiles like he is so proud he pulled this off without us guessin'. Mama just looks relieved that it's something she might enjoy after all.

I'm just beside myself. *This is too good to be true.* "Dinner theater? You mean we get to eat and watch a play at the same time?"

Adriana looks at me again.

The maître d', as Mama calls him, shows us to our table up near the stage. Once we're all seated, they bring us girls 7 UPs with bright red syrup and cherries on top. It's called a Shirley Temple. I'm watchin' the ruby red syrup swirl into the 7 UP. "Hey, my favorite color."

"What, clear?" Adriana says.

I just ignore her.

Then they bring out cherry Cokes for the guys, called Roy Rogers. Now Daddy finally gets to tell us what this is all about.

"Well, gang, I have just been promoted from Deputy Ranger to Head Ranger of Indian Lake State Park. So, I thought this would be a fun way to celebrate."

We all cheer and clang our glasses together in a toast for Daddy. Mama lets out one of her great whistles that I wish I could do, but can't, on account of losin' too much wind through my front teeth.

While we're all congratulatin' Daddy, the waiter brings us plates of spaghetti and puts them on the red-and-white checked tablecloth, which kind of goes along with this whole Wild West deal, but it works for us Italians, too.

The lights begin to go down real slow, and music starts to play, and my stomach is so excited to see what the actors are gonna look like. Suddenly, a girl, not much bigger'n me, bursts out on the stage and startles the daylights outta me by firin' a rifle. For a second I'm thinkin' it's real and she's gonna kill us all. Then I remember it's just a play, and I sit back again and relax. Now Adriana's watchin' me like a hawk watches its prey.

"What?" I whisper. "How was I supposed to know it was part of the play?"

"Gee, A. J., do you think the name of the play has any clues in it?" She finally looks away.

Now that things are rollin', I am just enjoyin' every single thing: the actors, the costumes, the props. I am so amazed by this "Little Miss Sure Shot." She is so good, she can outshoot anyone who takes her on. She even gets to travel with Colonel Cody's Wild West Show. By intermission, I feel like I want to be just like Annie Oakley and do somethin' better than any boy, like she does with her rifle.

During intermission, you can either stay and have dessert or wander around for a few minutes. Since dessert turns out to be coconut cream custard, I talk Benji into goin' explorin' with me instead. Coconut is one of those things that should really just stay up in those tall trees where we don't have to smell it, look at it, or eat it.

I can hardly wait to go snoop around this old place and maybe even spy on the actors to see what costumes they're climbin' into for part two.

We sneak down this long hallway and find a back room, like an overflow dressing room full of old theater photos and costumes. It's too tempting to resist the costumes. I throw a feather boa around my neck and pretend I'm an actress. Benji comes across a tall hat like Abe Lincoln's, and puts it on. It's like we're in our own little play that no one is watchin' but me and Benji.

Off in the corner there's a candy bar machine with those little windows showin' all the different candy bars you get to pick from. I sashay my way over to take a look. My favorite candy bar just happens to be the kind with chocolate and caramel mixed together, and wouldn't you know it, it's starin' right at me. Benji and me both stand here lookin' at it, wishin' we had a dime. Then I notice how close those little windows are to the slot where the stuff comes out, and I imagine myself reachin' right up inside there and grabbin' that candy bar.

"Hey, Benji, why don't you reach up there and grab that candy bar for us." Benji's arm is much smaller than mine, so it only makes sense he does the reachin' and grabbin'.

"Don't you have to put money in there?"

"Naw, it's probably free for the actors and little kids. Besides, we didn't get dessert like everyone else."

"Oh, yeah." So, Benji reaches his little arm up there as far as he can.

"I can't get it, A. J. I don't feel any candy bars up here."

Now I'm gettin' a little nervous about someone comin' to find us. "Okay, Benji, pull it back out."

"I can't, A. J. It's stuck."

Benji must've turned his arm a different angle from how it went in.

Now I'm feelin' really nervous. Just as I'm tryin' to pull Benji's arm out, who but Daddy comes in lookin' for us. This is not good. Benji's squattin' here in this big top hat, and his entire arm's missin' all the way up to his shoulder like the machine had just sucked it right up.... *Hey, maybe that's what we could say....*

"Well, here you two are. What in the world ... Benji, what are you doing?" Daddy looks from Benji to me. I'm all wrapped up in this purple boa, tryin' with all my might to get Benji's arm out of the slot.

"A. J. said it was free for actors and little kids, Daddy, but now my arm is stuck and won't come out, and I didn't even get the candy."

"Is that so? Well, I think A. J. is going to get more than a candy bar out of this deal—like the privilege of picking up every candy wrapper in the entire state park." Then he yanks Benji's little arm out of there so fast, and he gives me a glare that makes me feel like I wish I really had been adopted by a pack of wolves like Wolf Boy. Maybe then I would've been brave enough to have stuck my own arm up there, and could've just chewed it off when it got stuck, before Daddy found me.

"Take off those silly things and get your sorry behinds back to your seats. We'll deal with this later at home." Then he turns to me. "And we *will* deal with it, A. J."

We leave our costumes in a crumpled heap on the floor by the candy machine and hustle back down the hall. I find our table and sit my sorry behind back down, wonderin' what got into me that made me do such a thing, and right in the middle of Daddy's celebration. Sometimes I think I must be possessed.

Exit Stage Right

The second half of the play isn't as good as the first half, probably because every time I look over at Benji, he's rubbin' his sore arm. I can't stop thinkin' about wolves. I'm gonna really wish I was one by Wednesday night. Wolves don't have to go to confession and explain things like this to Father Patrick.

After the final curtain, I stay behind to get Miss Annie's autograph. My family goes on ahead to the dock while I wait in line. Mama sails past me in all of her Hollywood flair, sunglasses, headscarf, and Poppy Pink lips. "Don't be long, dahlin'," she calls back to me, in her deep Miss Loren voice. Then she laughs to the wind and leaves me behind to get all the strange looks. Mama's the only person I know who can't just *walk* past a crowd of people.

I have never gotten any real autographs before—well, except my mama's—but that doesn't count. While Miss Annie is signin' my play program, I notice some of the actors whisperin' and lookin' over at me. *Either they heard about the candy machine, or they're makin' fun of my dramatic mother.* Then a few of them walk over to me.

"Was that your mom who just went by?"

"U-h-h … yeah." *Thanks, Mama.*

"Do you mind if we ask what her name is?"

I should know better, but I can't help myself. "Sophia … her name is Sophia … and she loves to scout for new risin' stars in the theater. Well, bye." Then I walk across the street and climb into our boat.

"Umm … Daddy," I say, lookin' back at the playhouse, "you might want to gun it outta here real fast."

"Why's that, A. J.?"

"Look …"

The entire cast is runnin' like a stampede of cows toward the dock, yellin,' "Sophia, Sophia!"

"What did you say to them, A. J.?" Daddy asks.

"Well … they asked what Mama's name was … so, I told 'em."

Adriana shakes her head. "Can't we go anywhere without you causing a scene?"

Mama doesn't seem to mind a bit. She just waves to all of them and blows a kiss as we speed off into the sunset.

3

Sisters, Saints, and Sinners

There is one question that will follow me into eternity because I'm too embarrassed to ask anyone in the church about it. *Why would God make a flower as pretty as a daisy smell like dog doo?* I will never forget the first time I stuck my nose right in the middle of one and nearly died. I felt like I'd been tricked. Then I wondered if God does that for fun and laughs every time someone smells one for their first time. Maybe I'll work up the nerve to ask one of the nuns tonight at catechism.

Every Wednesday night is catechism for us kids. Our main church is St. Peter's Parish, but that's when we're livin' in town. When we're on the island, we just go downlake to Our Lady of the Lake. It's way smaller, and you don't have to dress all holy to go there. We like it better than St. Peter's. One reason is, the people don't "shush" you when you're whisperin' too loud, and the other is, it has clear windows. Daddy says that way when the message goes long, he has a nice view of the water to get him through. He also said the reason they put stained glass in the big churches is to force you to look at the pulpit so the priest can't tell when he's lost everybody. Mama says Daddy needs to repent for tellin' us that.

I don't think God minds me lookin' out those windows at the lake. Sometimes when the sunlight is hittin' the water just so, it looks like tiny diamonds dancin' across the waves. I may not hear everything the priest is sayin', but I'm sure thinkin' about God.

On the way to catechism, we swing by the gas dock to refill our gas tank. Buzz is a foul-talkin' ex-sailor who pumps our gas. Daddy calls him "a crusty ol' cuss." He sits in a saggy wicker chair on the end of the dock with his bare potbelly hangin' out over his belt. He also has a fat hula dancer tattooed right on his stomach. I think she used to be skinny and danced the hula when Buzz flexed his stomach muscles. Now she looks more like she's doin' the limbo—the way his big fat belly sticks out.

Buzz acts all put out whenever we tie up. "S'pose you'll be wantin' some gas?" as though we have a choice of somethin' besides gas at the gas dock. Then, he heaves himself out of his chair and waddles over to the pump with his cigarette hangin' from his bottom lip. "Finally get a nice hot day, and them bleepin' clouds gotta show up an' turn this place into a bleepin' sauna."

I'm worried this place is gonna turn into an inferno if he doesn't toss his cigarette in the water before pumpin' our gas.

It's always about the weather with Buzz. It's either too bleepin' hot or too bleepin' cold, never just right. He owns the gas dock, so you'd think he'd want your business. He treats you like he's doin' you a favor by takin' your money. "I s'pose yer gonna want change now, aren't ya?"

Sometimes I just feel like sayin', "Good grief, Buzz, why did you pick a job you hate in a place where you can't stand the weather?" Daddy says it would be fun to get Buzz and Grandma Juliana together sometime. Maybe after spendin' a day with Grandma Juliana, his gas dock life wouldn't look so bad after all.

I love my catechism teacher, Sister Abigail. She is such a nice nun. She's been teachin' us all about this nun in Calcutta called Mother Teresa, who takes care of really sick and dying people. Sister Abigail says this lady really has a heart for the things of God. Sister Abigail's favorite word is *grace*. She says if that's the only thing she ever helps us to understand about God, then she's done her job.

Tonight she gave us a writing assignment to help us understand what grace is like. She had us pretend we were havin' a really bad day—so bad that we turn into bad guys to deal with our sorry lives. Then she had us write down all the horrible things we could possibly think of doin' in one day if we'd really turned into bad guys. She said to use our imaginations.

So, here's what I wrote,

I stole a fire engine from the Squawkomish fire station and dressed up in all the equipment, then drove around our block with the sirens on. I turned on the loud speaker and yelled at the neighborhood bully, who always plays his dumb music too loud, "Turn it down." But he wouldn't, so I squirted him with the fire hose just as he reached to turn his radio up louder, and accidentally electrocuted him, causin' sparks to catch his house on fire, which I was able to put out just in time to rescue his dog, but unfortunately the kid didn't make it.

Then I went to Saddlemyer's Variety Store and accidentally drove the fire engine through their front window. Since no one was around, I took all of their candy, Fizzies, and a clown costume. I put on the costume and ran through the library as Chuckles the Clown, yellin' and laughin' as loud as I could, then ran out the back door.

I wore the costume over to Buzz's gas dock where he was sleepin' in his old chair, and I painted a big red smile on his face. Then I stole a fancy yacht from the gas dock with the keys in it and drove like a madman in my clown costume all over the lake 'til I crashed it into ...

"Okay, class, stop writing."

Sister Abigail pretended to be the judge and had each of us tell our offenses to the classroom jury.

I got to go first: "Stealin' a fire truck, murder, breaking and entering, stealin' goods, disruptin' the public, annoying someone, stealin' a boat, destruction of … I didn't get to finish that one."

"Okay," Sister Abigail said, "now let's hear from the jury."

The class all yelled, "Guilty, guilty, guilty."

"Now," Sister Abigail said, "write what you think the sentence and punishment should be for your crimes, and save them for when you go privately to the judge's chamber. While you're waiting to be called out, I want each of you to think of all the things you will no longer be able to do if you are convicted of your crimes, places you will never go and loved ones you will never see again … family, friends, pets."

We all sat there thinkin' it over. It felt kind of real when I thought of leavin' Sailor and my hamster, Ruby, forever. Who would feed them, who would love them like I do?

Sister Abigail called us out one at a time, then sent each kid off to confession afterwards, so we didn't get to hear what she said to anyone else. My turn finally came.

"Angelina Degulio, how do you plead to the charges you've been accused of?"

"Guilty." I did feel kind of bad.

"What is your sentence and punishment?"

"To rot in prison with no parole, forty lashes right off the bat, then solitary confinement on Alcatraz, surrounded by sharks—in case I ever try to escape."

"Angelina, as the judge, I agree that you deserve your

stated sentence and punishment, however … an innocent man has just informed me that he will be serving your sentence and taking your punishment for you, in full."

"Who?" I gasped. I looked around wonderin' who would ever volunteer for this.

"His name is Jesus. You, Angelina, may go free."

That is why I like Sister Abigail better than Sister Mary Ellen at St. Peter's Parish.

Sister Mary Ellen is really into this whole suffering thing. Her favorite saying is, "Until you have something worth dying for, you have nothing worth living for." She reads us these stories from Foxe's *Book of Martyrs.* I think she's hopin' to turn some of us into good little martyrs when we grow up. I'm not sure I want to be quite that holy. She says she wants the stories to spark passion in our souls, but so far all they've sparked in me is nightmares. Mama says if I have any more dreams of bein' fed to the lions, she's gonna have a talk with Sister Mary Ellen.

Before we came to the island this summer, Sister Mary Ellen gave us her writing assignment. She said to write about the things in life that stir our hearts and what kind of saints we might become if we follow our Calling. The winning author would get to ride the float in the St. Peter's Parish Patron Saint's Parade when Bishop Bartholomew comes to visit at the end of summer. (Daddy calls him Bishop Bart, because he is really short and should have a much shorter name for someone so small.)

I wasn't sure if this was the kind of contest I even wanted to win, but here's what I wrote,

One thing that stirs my heart is the poem "If," which has been hangin' above my bed since before I could even spell it. When you have words like that hangin' over you day and night, how can you grow up expectin' to be a nobody?

And, the other thing that stirs my heart is watchin' a Billy Graham crusade on TV when they sing "Just as I Am," and all the people get up from their seats and go forward in front of everybody to say, "Hey, I'm a big fat sinner and I know it, and, boy, could I use a Savior right now."

I would like to become "The Patron Saint for Stirring Up Boring People." Life should be more than just pumpin' gas and complainin' about the weather. Some people really bother me because they just sit there and never wonder about these things. It just makes you want to shake 'em and say, "Wake up. Don't just sit there. God gave you a brain ... do something. Make something of yourself so the rest of us don't have to sit around and watch boring people like you. But if all you want to do in life is sit around and never look for your Calling, then go ahead, but don't come to our church or you'll just mess it up for the rest of us who have better things to do than listen to you whine about your dumb, boring life."

By A. J. Degulio

I didn't win. That's okay. It kind of scared me to think of ridin' the float with Bishop Bart anyway. What if I tripped and fell off right in the middle of the parade when I was throwin' candy to all the little kids? Besides, we'll be right here at our cabin during the St. Peter's Parish Patron Saint's Parade anyway, and I wouldn't want to go just to embarrass myself like that in front of the whole town.

4

True Confessions

I'm waitin' my turn for confession when Sister Abigail comes and sits in the front pew beside me. I'm kind of afraid to ask, but I need to talk to her about a *family matter.*

"Excuse me, Sister Abigail, can I ... um, ask you something?"

"Yes, Angelina, what is it, dear?"

I lean in real close so no one else can hear me. "Sister, I was just wondering ... is speakin' with a Southern accent a sin?"

She looks at me with her headdress cocked to one side, and says, "Why, child, I don't believe the Lord would consider any accent a sin if that's the language He's placed within you."

"Thank you, Sister," I whisper, with the highest respect in my voice. *That's one less sin I'll have to confess tonight.* I didn't tell her I wasn't from the South or that I was a late bloomer in acquiring my Southern language.

I don't want to dishonor our family or drive Mama insane like she accuses me of, but I will still talk Southern in my head for fear of losin' my accent entirely. If I can secretly hold onto it 'til I have my own family, I can raise all my children with that beautiful language and hear it all around my house. We'll just have to put the kibosh on it when their Grandma Sophia comes to visit.

Confession is like my least favorite place to go. I get so scared in that dark closet waiting for the little window to slide open. I'm just shakin' like a jackhammer, rehearsin' my sins over and over. My worst sin by far is Ruby Jean. All because I walked into that pet store just to look. That's when I spotted her, the most beautiful albino hamster I'd ever laid eyes on. She was pure white, just like she'd been bathed in Clorox bleach. I even considered namin' her Clorox, but she also had these ruby red eyes to die for. That's why I decided on Ruby, and I added the middle name Jean for the Southern effect. I begged my daddy to let me get her, but the answer was, "No, I've got seven mouths to feed already, and I don't need a rodent to add to it."

I figured it wouldn't put Daddy out in any way if I just rode my bike back to the pet store, paid for Ruby and her food with my own allowance, and rode her home in my pocket. I didn't see the harm in just smuggling her out to the island with me and keepin' her out in the shed. It can't be a burden to them if they don't know she's here. Besides, I've already named her, and I don't think pet stores will let you return pets once you've named them.

Father Patrick is taking confession from Jorgan Junker on the other side of the confessional. He must've done a lot of sinning lately 'cause it is takin' forever. I am dyin' to know what kind of sins Jorgan Junker's been up to, so I lean my ear up to the wall to see if I can hear anything. Zippo. At least I know no one can hear mine either.

I get real antsy and start to tinker with the knotholes in the wall. I find a hole where the knot's loose and push on it with my pointer finger. Holy smokes—the knot pops right through into the priest's chamber. I have a ring on my finger, and when I go to pull my finger back out, the ring shimmies up my knuckle and I can't, for the life of me, get my finger back outta that hole. I just start prayin', *You gotta help me here, Lord. My finger's stickin' right through into that chamber where Father Patrick will be takin' my confession any minute now.*

I tug and pull, but it just won't budge. Then I hear Father Patrick shift over to my side. He slides the little window back.

Oh dear Jesus, make that darkness in there so dark it hides my finger; make my finger invisible.

Then in the quiet, clear as day, comes the thought, *Lay your finger down and keep it still.* My finger is pointing straight out in front of Father Patrick's nose, so I just bend it down, lay it to rest, and begin my confession:

"Bless me, Father, for I have sinned...."

Father Patrick seems pretty bored with my usual list: sneakin' Kool-Aid, plotting revenge on my sister, makin' fun of Tommy Jacob's buckteeth. He doesn't even flinch over the candy bar story. But when I get to Ruby, *that* seems to get his attention. I tell him I smuggled a hamster home after my parents told me no. This is the first time he's ever turned his head over something I've confessed.

I was worried I might run out of Rosary beads doin' my penance for Ruby, but turns out, it only costs me three Hail Marys. He must think I've already been found out, but it might become more clear to him when I make the same confession next week.

For the moment I have a bigger problem deciding whether or not to confess that my finger's stuck in the hole. Just as Father Patrick is turning away, I give it one last tug. I have worked up such a sweat worryin' that the ring flings right off my finger into Father Patrick's chamber. I wonder if he will somehow put it all together one day when he finds my ring and that pine knot layin' right beside one another on his floor. I just thank the Lord for givin' me mercy.

I will tell you, when you go in there with your soul all filled up with black spots and come out white as snow, that's about the best feelin' in the whole world.

It's the same feelin' I had when I took my First Holy Communion. I felt like I'd been dunked in Clorox from the top of my lacey white veil, down to the soles of my ruffly white socks. I appeared at that altar like a vision out of heaven. If someone had stuck a pair of wings on my back, I'd have looked like an angel in patent leather shoes. But confession makes you feel that way on the inside, too.

Mama says goin' to confession is like puttin' Clorox on mold. Zap. She says Clorox is a cure-all for just about anything dirty, but when it comes to sin, the only cure is Jesus. And don't I know it.

When I get home, I tell Mama that Sister Abigail said speakin' with a Southern accent is not a sin.

"Listen up, toots," she says, "if you want to play hardball with me, I will go to the pope in Rome if I have to in order to prove that a full-blooded Italian, Roman Catholic nine-year-old girl, born and raised in the Northwest, who insists on speaking with a Southern accent and driving her mother to the brink of insanity, is dishonoring to the family. Which, in my book, makes it a sin."

I've decided to just let it go for now.

My sins range from bad, to really bad, like Ruby. The most common one is sneakin' the Kool-Aid out from the kitchen to eat straight out of the package. Mama has forbidden us to touch it unless we put it into a pitcher of water the way it was intended. But that's not half as fun as eatin' it straight and makin' your mouth pucker. The only thing that beats Kool-Aid, hands down, is Fizzies. You're supposed to put one tablet in a big glass of water, and it makes a nice fizzy drink. Now, you put one of those tablets in your mouth straight, and you feel like your tongue is gonna explode right through the roof of your mouth.

We used to have Fizzie contests to see who could keep the Fizzie on their tongue the longest. That was 'til Mama caught on. She wondered why she couldn't keep those things in the cupboard for more than a day. Then she walked in on our last Fizzie contest. There we were, all five kids, with our tongues hangin' out and bright red Fizzies sizzlin' all over them.

"That's it," she yells. "This must be another one of those dominant genes from your father's side of the family that causes bright red tongues and insanity among its offspring. Now stop this idiotic behavior before I drop the whole bunch of ya off at the zoo—and I don't mean for a visit."

That was the last we saw of the Fizzies. We've learned to be more careful with the Kool-Aid. We also take turns sneakin' it so we can spread the sins out a little and they don't all fall on one soul. Sometimes when the guilt is weighing heavy, I will bury half of the package for a guilt offering. When that doesn't help, I just resort to eating red blackberries. The pucker is a little too strong, but at least it's guilt free.

One of my bigger sins was takin' pop cans around the neighborhood collecting money for the Bluebirds of America, then goin' to the store to buy candy with it. My conscience won't let me get away with that kind of thing. It was over a year ago, but sometimes I still lay awake at night thinkin' about it. When I'm older and have a good job, I may just go back to all of those sweet old people who gave us money and pay them back. I hope they live long enough to see that day. They deserve restitution for trusting children who were not worthy of their trust. We've been learnin' about restitution in catechism. Restitution is about sins you can be forgiven for, but sometimes you still have to pay the price for what you did. The sins of consequences. I think this may be one of those kinds of sins.

I am prayin' that God will give me mercy over Ruby. I think He knows that it will tear my heart out if I have to give Ruby Jean away. At least it gives me someone besides Mama to talk Southern to. As I'm layin' in bed tonight, Mama and Daddy are out on the porch swing, and I can hear every word they're sayin' through my open window.

"Sonny, tell me how that child of yours comes off speaking with a Southern accent. Why can't she just speak a normal kid lingo, like Pig Latin?"

"Soph, A. J. may be a little on the quirky side, but she has a tender heart, and I don't ever want to see her lose that. If a Southern accent is the worst thing to come out of that kid, then so be it."

I wonder if Mama will decide not to take me to the pope in Rome since Daddy said that.

I keep secret diaries on almost everyone on this island. I love bein' a journalist. I'm torn between bein' a veterinarian or a newspaper journalist when I grow up. I find that people can sound very interesting on paper.

Even the most boring of people can sound fascinating when I write about them in my journals. Take the relatives who come to visit our landlord, Mr. Mueller. He has some of the strangest relatives I could ever hope to meet. Whenever I even start to get bored, I go lookin' for Mr. Mueller. I usually find him out watering his flowers.

I'll say, "Good mornin', Mr. Mueller. Awful fine day, isn't it?"

"Umm-hmm," he'll mumble back.

"Nice garden you have there."

"Umm-hmm."

"Plannin' on any visitors soon?"

Sometimes it's just, "Nope." But on a lucky day he'll say, "E'spectin' a few relatives this week."

That's all it takes for me to run home and dig out my diary entitled, "MR. MUELLER'S RELATIVES." Then I keep my ears perked for a day or two, 'til I hear his old boat engine whining its way to the mainland to pick them up.

Mr. Mueller is a grumpy old man most of the time, but only because of a broken heart. The year before we started comin' out here, he lived on this happy little island with his wife, Scarlett. It was just the two of 'em then. One day in winter, his wife was driving home from town with her groceries. It was snowin' out, and there was ice on the roads. Mrs. Mueller crossed over a bridge and slid right into a potato truck comin' the other way. There were potatoes rollin' all over the road, and floatin' down the river. Mr. Mueller lost his only true love that day.

So when Mr. Mueller acts grumpy to me, I just smile at him and try and cheer up his day. There's little more you can do for someone with a broken heart. A smile can't cheer up his whole life, but maybe a few minutes of his day. Every once in a while I will say somethin' that will make him smile. That cheers up my day because I know that, for a split second, he forgot about his dead wife.

When I hear that boat motor whining back toward the island, I put my journal and good writing pen into my duffel bag and scoot to the other side of the island before they arrive. I get myself positioned on a bank just above the boat dock that they're gonna pull up to. My heart always starts to beat faster just waitin' to see who's gonna climb off that boat. Here's what I wrote about the bunch that came yesterday:

July 13, 1968
by Journalist, A. J. Degulio

Mr. Mueller's relatives came today from, get this ... OKLAHOMA. I feel like I'm in heaven up here on this bank, with that sweet Oklahoma chatter driftin' up to me like incense (not the stinky kind Adriana burns). I wonder if they'll be able to tell that I'm a fake Southerner. I'm watchin' 'em all unload, and all I see is a swarm of fancy-lookin' women with bright red nails and high-heeled sandals. I'm catchin' a few names that I would trade my name for in a heartbeat—names like Aunt Rebecca and Auntie Charlotte.

I don't see any men at all, but there's a tribe of little kids. I see one older boy who looks about sixteen or seventeen, around Adriana's age. Here we go again.

Well, gotta go now. I can't wait to see these Okies close up, so I'm gonna wander down by the cabins and see if I can't lay a Southern "howdy" on one or two of 'em.

Later, A. J.

Reporting live for *Island News*

I love journaling about island romances. Poor Adriana gets crushed every time. The boys she meets out here always leave with a chunk of her heart. Every time one leaves, we all get to watch her mope around until the next one comes along. Before ya know it, she's over the old one and on to the next. She reminds me of one of those floozies who sit on the piano in the Western movies and wink at all the guys. I don't think nice girls should act like that.

Adriana's not allowed to kiss boys, but now that I've seen some of her diary pages, I've got the dirt on her. I was just gettin' to the good part last night when Dino—the snitch—ran out to the dock yellin', "Adriana, A. J.'s getting into your diaria." Which to everyone else sounded like, "A. J.'s getting into your *diarrhea.*"

Everyone got a good laugh out of that except Adriana, who threatened to break my new Andy Williams record album if I get into her diary again. I've decided to take a different route with Adriana. I'm going to stalk her and record all the details of her island romances in my key-lock diary, and I'll hide the key where she'll never find it. By the time we're off of this island, I should have enough material to write an entire novel. I am not above blackmail when it comes to my sister.

5

Juniper Beach

This morning I'm headed over to Mr. Mueller's compound to check up on the newcomers. I never did get up the nerve to try my Southern accent out on any of those folks yesterday. Just as I'm comin' around the bend on the trail, I nearly run right into a tall sandy-haired boy. He looks as surprised to see me as I am to see him. I'm so flustered, I just turn and run the other way. I can't believe I did that. I will feel so stupid if I ever see him again.

I'm usually not shy unless someone is close to my own age, a boy, or very cute. This one is all three. I don't remember seein' him gettin' off the boat. Couldn't say for sure how old he is. Looks a little older than me. Maybe him and J. R. could become friends. J. R. gets tired of playin' with Benji and Dino. He'll be happy to know there's someone here closer to his own age.

Me and J. R. hang out together when J. R. feels like bein' around a girl. But sometimes I can tell he'd just like to have a guy to hang out with. The two younger ones are always off fishin' together, but J. R.'s at that age where he'd rather fish by himself than put up with us.

He used to invite me to go along, but not anymore. He got real mad at me for lettin' his fish go free after it took him all morning to catch it. There it was swimmin' in a tiny bucket of water on our way back to the dock, soon to be turned into breakfast. I just couldn't help myself from liftin' that bucket over the back of the boat and pourin' him back. It was quite a shock once we got back to the dock and J. R. peered inside that empty bucket. I'll never forget the look on his face.... But I'll never forget that fish swimmin' off to freedom either.

I have a secret place to go when I feel like bein' alone. The first summer we were here, I discovered a sandy cove where no one goes but me. It's well hidden along the far side of the island, and you have to go through a tangle of blackberry sticker bushes to get to it. It is the only white sandy beach on the island. I can sit for hours in the sun and sift that white sand through my toes. It's so soft and fine, it reminds me of coffee creamer. Makes me wonder if someone didn't barge in a ton of coffee creamer and dump it right here on my beach. I love that stuff so much, I eat it straight from the jar with a spoon. I'm actually thinkin' of plantin' a palm tree along the shore someday. Maybe I could tie a little blanket around it every winter 'til we come back in the summer.

I have decided to name my cove Juniper Beach. I

don't really know what a juniper looks like, and that's the part that bothers Mama.

"A. J.," she says, "you can't name a beach Juniper Beach if there are no junipers on it. There are no junipers on this entire island for that matter."

"Oh, Mama, I know, but I just really like the way it sounds. I guess I could change it to Coffee Creamer Shores."

Mama raises one eyebrow and glances over at Daddy like she's blamin' him for oddball genes again. "Never mind," Mama says. "Juniper Beach is the better choice. Stick with that one, kiddo."

I love to go to my beach just to think, or pray, or dive for old bottles. I have found all kinds of little blue glass medicine bottles. I have a whole row of them on my windowsill above my bed. I'm half thinkin' a doctor may have lived here at one time. Daddy thinks it was probably more like a band of pirates who got stranded on this island and were too drunk to swim to shore. My daddy should be a writer. He comes up with the greatest stories. I love to listen to the "Park Mysteries" he makes up about bein' a park ranger at Indian Lake State Park. Mama says that's who I get my crazy ideas from.

I love a good mystery, especially tryin' to figure out "who done it." Sometimes we'll sit by the fire pit and Daddy will get us all goin' on one of his stories, then make us guess who done it. We tell him how many clues we think we need and whoever guesses with the fewest clues wins. The reason I like this game so much is because I usually win. Me and Daddy think so much alike, I can pretty much guess which way he's goin' with his characters. Daddy acts so surprised every time I guess it right, and he tells everyone I was cheatin' by readin' his mind.

I used to fall for everything Daddy ever told us. My sister still makes fun of me for believin' his story about Falling Rock. Bein' raised on cowboys and Indians didn't help either. Every time we drove up to the mountains, Daddy would point out the sign that said "Watch for Falling Rock." He told us Falling Rock was a little Indian brave who wandered from his tribe when he was small and is still lost up in those mountains tryin' to find his way home. I always hoped to see him pop up from behind one of those big boulders with a tomahawk and a head full of feathers. I would imagine myself as the little white girl who found him and brought him back to his tribe. Then they would capture me and make me part of their tribe. But I didn't mind because me and Falling Rock were secretly in love, and I grew up to become his beautiful Indian princess. And I never had to see Adriana ever again.

Me and Sailor cut over to my secret blackberry sticker trail and make a run for the beach. It's too hard to spy on folks when you've got a big hairy dog following you around. Sailor loves to swim after sticks. He's carrying one in his mouth right now, just hopin' we are on our way to play fetch in the water.

One thing that's nice, the sun rises on my beach. If we get there real early, we can watch it come up, but today, it's already up and on its way. It feels like it's gonna be good and hot by noon. I start throwin' sticks for Sailor, and he plunges in that cold water like it doesn't faze him one bit. Our friends on the mainland have a dog named Wolfie who actually swims underwater and tries to catch fish all day long. I think he's only caught one fish in his whole life, but he keeps tryin'. Wolfie is the only dog I've ever known who can hold its breath underwater. I've tried to teach Sailor to dive for things, but he likes to keep his head above water.

I'm lookin' around, thinkin' how proud I am of my beach, when the next thing I know, I'm staring right into two clear blue eyes. And they don't belong to Sailor.

Just my luck, they belong to the boy I nearly bumped into earlier. I'm thinkin,' *Hey, what are you doin' on my beach?*

Then he smiles at me. "Howdy."

My heart just skips a beat over the way he says "howdy," with a true Oklahoma accent. Do I dare speak Southern back and risk makin' a fool of myself? Or just say "hello," and regret it for the rest of my life?

I can't help blushin'. "Howdy yerself."

He doesn't flinch an inch over hearin' my accent. He sits down on the log next to me, as though he owns the whole beach himself.

"You're the one I saw on the trail earlier. Are you stayin' out here on the island?" he asks.

"My family's stayin' over yonder in Papoose," I reply, much bolder.

This time he laughs, like maybe he's on to me bein' a fake. "I have a brother, looks to be 'bout your age," I quickly add. "How old are you?"

"Thirteen, almost fourteen."

"My brother J. R. just turned fourteen. He'll be happy to meet you. Maybe he can take you fishin' with him sometime. You like fishin'?"

"Sure do. You tell your brother to come by in the mornin' if he wants to go fishin'."

"Which cabin are you stayin' at?" I ask.

"Big Chief, with my grandpa and my brother. My mama and my aunts are stayin' at Pocahontas with all the cousins."

"Mr. Mueller's yer grandpa then?" I wonder why I've never seen him on the island before.

"Yes, ma'am."

I can't believe he called me ma'am. Nobody's ever called me ma'am. "What's your name?" I ask.

"Danny. Danny Morgan. And yours?"

"Just call me A. J."

"Okay, A. J.," he says, *real* Southernly. That's the first time I've ever heard my name said right, and I like the way it sounds.

"How long y'all stayin' out here?" I ask, half hopin' he'll say all summer."

"'Bout three weeks."

"I don't remember seein' your family on the island before."

"My family works the fields during summer in Oklahoma. We usually come to visit over Christmas. There's not as much work to do on the farm when it's cold and wet."

"So, how'd you get to come this summer?"

"Well, my mama an' her sisters all decided on havin'

some reunion, so they told my daddy she was goin', with or without him. He told 'em all to go on ahead without him 'cause he didn't want to be the only rooster stuck in the middle of some hen party. Then he told my mama she might as well take me an' my brother, too, so we could rest up for all the hay bailin' that'll be waitin' for us when we get back. Y'all come here every summer, A. J.?"

"Yes, sir." I just had to try that out once myself. "My daddy's the ranger at Indian Lake State Park. When school starts up in the fall, we head back to our house in town. Me and Daddy would love to live out here year-round, but my mama says she likes goin' back and forth so she doesn't have time to go crazy in either place."

"I sure would like to live here myself. I can't see ever gettin' tired of this island. Oklahoma summers get *so* hot when we're workin' the fields. I'd give anything to just stay on with my grandpa. My brother plans to take on the farm one day, but me … I'm dreamin' of somethin' all together different."

I want to ask him what he's dreamin' of, but I change my mind. If he were to ask me what I dream about, I'd feel way too embarrassed to tell him that it's kissin' Little Joe Cartwright. So I change the subject. "I think I saw your brother comin' off the boat yesterday. I have a sister 'bout his age. Won't take long for her to find him."

"Well, if there's a girl on this island anywhere near his age, I bet Jason's already found her."

We both laugh just thinkin' about those two out there lookin' for each other.

"Well, I guess I'd better be gettin' back to see if

Grandpa needs any help. Some of those women can be mighty demandin' of him." He gets up to leave. "Nice meetin' you, A. J." Then he looks over at Sailor. "You, too, boy." He turns and walks down Juniper Beach toward the trail.

I sit on my beach with Sailor for a long time just thinkin' things over. I've decided that Danny Morgan is the only boy I might ever be willin' to share my beach with.

6

Saving Sailor

It's the middle of the night, and I just woke up feelin' like God tapped me on the shoulder. I'm lyin' here in bed with the moonlight streamin' through my window. There's a soft breeze, and I have this feelin' deep in my soul that Jesus is right here in this room with me, smilin' down from my ceiling. I lie here just smilin' back. Sometimes I think He must want somethin' more than just my long list of prayers, like maybe He just wants to hang around with me.

This is one of those nights where I was so tired when I went to bed, I didn't even say my prayers. I just said, "Ditto, Lord, from last night." I can only get away with that every other night.

My prayers get longer and longer every night that I actually pray. First, I pray the Lord's Prayer, then, "Now I lay me down to sleep, I pray the Lord my soul to keep." I stop right there and skip the "if I should die before I wake." That always gets me thinkin' too much and creeps me out. Then,

I pray for every family member, especially Adriana. I ask God to help her stop kissin' all those boys and wait for the right one. Then, I ask Him to save us from burglars, fires, and earthquakes. Then, I get to my pet list and the souls of all my dead animals. This can take so long I sometimes fall asleep before I get to the end of my list.

Animals have always been a struggle for me. I'm no longer permitted to go into pet stores, dog pounds, or animal shelters of any kind. I've been banned from just about every animal establishment there is, with the exception of the zoo.

All of that came about because of a trip we took to the dog pound for Adriana's sixteenth birthday last spring. My sister has always wanted a little peekapoo, probably because they are kind of prissy, like she is. Personally, I never much cared for poo dogs of any kind, especially poodles.

White french poodles are the *worst*. They're all shaved up except for those big poofs on top of their heads that look like giant cream puffs. Then they wear those fake diamond collars around their necks like they're somethin' special. If they only knew how dumb they looked, they might not prance around actin' so hoity-toity. They remind me of spoiled, snobby children, and why would you deliberately go out and look for one, let alone buy one?

Well, we looked up and down the rows and rows of cages until she found it, a shaggy little white mop that looked like somethin' you'd put on the end of a broomstick and dust your floors with. I could only take so much of that "yip, yip, yippin'," before I decided to wander off by myself. Along the back wall of the pound was a row of cages apart from the others. It suddenly hit me—these were the dogs on death row. They were next to go. I looked each dog in the eye and realized their lives would soon end for no good reason. Then I saw him. I stood in front of his cage just staring into his big sad eyes. Next thing I knew, he walked up to the door and lifted his paw toward me. That's when Mama and Daddy, and everyone else on the premises, heard a deep wailin' echo from the back of the pound. People came runnin' from all directions to find me clingin' to the front of the dog cage, sobbing, "Don't kill him, don't kill him, *don't kill him....*"

No one could pry my fingers loose from that cage. The pound warden came runnin' as well and was about to try and pull me away, when my daddy stopped him. "It's no use, sir." My daddy just shook his head. "You're going to have to sell us that dog."

"I'm sorry, mister, but this dog is not available for adoption. He's … uh … he's …"

"We know," Mama cut in, "but you'll have to make an exception. You see, our daughter here suffers from animal compassion. If you don't let us adopt that dog, she won't let go of that cage. And if you try to put that dog down … well, you may as well put that child down with it, because she will die from a broken heart … sir."

Now, I don't remember too many times in my life when someone tried to stand up to my mama, but when it comes to her children, you might as well just wake up a mean mother bear with five cubs at her side.

I have a feelin' that warden could see it in her eyes. He just scratched his head, lookin' puzzled, but in the end he did the wise thing. "Well, ma'am, guess I don't see a problem with making an exception here."

My daddy slowly pried my fingers free from the cage door and let the warden by to get the dog out. I overheard the warden say to my mama, "Ma'am, you might not want to take your daughter into these kind of places anymore, if you know what I mean."

I don't remember much else, but I do remember that instead of leavin' with a small white peekapoo, we were walkin' that big hairy dog out the front door to freedom.

Somehow in all of the commotion, another family had snatched up the little white mop. I tried to apologize to my sister. "I'm sorry about your poo, Adriana. I didn't mean to wreck your birthday."

Adriana just flicked her hair back like she didn't even hear me and kept on walkin'. That's when Mama put her arm around my shoulder and whispered, "She'll be okay, kiddo. We'll buy her that dress she likes." Sometimes that's all it takes for Mama to let me know she understands my strange ways. That's what I love most about Mama. But from that day on, nothin' was quite the same between me and Adriana.

As I'm lyin' here with Sailor sprawled across my bed, his big furry head on my pillow, and my arms wrapped around his neck, I suddenly see Mama and Daddy in my doorway. The hall light's shinin' behind them, so they can't see that my eyes are open, but I can see them. I can see them standin' there together lookin' in on me and Sailor … just lookin', and smilin' at us. Now I have Mama, Daddy, and Jesus all smilin' at me, and it feels so good. As soon as they walk away, Adriana appears in my doorway. I have never seen anyone look at me so cold in all my life. That sweet, warm peace I was feelin' just fades away.

I have a big project this morning that I've been wantin' to finish for a long time. It's a sign for my critter cemetery. I finally got the red paint I needed for the lettering. Now all these animals will have a proper sign marking their place of rest. When it comes to animals, Mama says I'm overboard. But she lets me stay that way, and has even pointed out that it may very well be my Divine Calling.

She stopped by this morning and said, "A. J., it won't surprise me if I get to heaven only to find you in charge of the entire animal kingdom." She says the good Lord is always looking for someone faithful enough to put a Calling on.

Sister Abigail says that if you can be faithful in the little things, then He'll trust you with the big things, and He may even let you help Him run His kingdom. That's one reason I have my critter cemetery here on the island. When Sister Abigail told us about how Mother Teresa in Calcutta helps all those poor dying people in India to die with dignity and gives them a proper burial, well, I decided to have the same type of setup here for animals.

I have always felt horrible seein' a dead animal lyin' all alone on the side of the road or a bird just lyin' there on its back with its feet stickin' straight up. So, I bring anything dead on the island to my cemetery, and I bury it myself. Then I make a stick cross to lie on top of its grave, pick a few flowers, and have a small funeral. I feel it gives honor to God to know that someone has taken the time to care for one of His fallen creatures. I sometimes even go as far as to bury dead bees or beetles that I come across, just to stay faithful to the little things.

My brothers know all about my sacred burial site, and none of them are allowed to step foot in it because it's too hard to tell where all the dead animals are buried once the flowers die. Daddy has let them know that they will have him to contend with if they cross that line. There are plenty of other places on the island for them to play and build their forts, and my cemetery is off-limits.

I finally finish the last letter on my sign and stand back to look at it:

WELCOME TO
A. J.'S HAVEN OF REST—
DEATH WITH DIGNITY
FOR DEAD ANIMALS

I plan to post this right at my cemetery entrance next to my St. Francis of Assisi statue. Grandma Juliana is really into these saint statues. She has one for just about everything you could think of. It's kind of a known family secret that Grandma Juliana is … well … the way Daddy tried to explain it to me in my terms was, "When it comes to Grandma Juliana's mind, it's like the wheel is still turning, but the hamster is missing." Mama calls it senile. For instance, we got a call from the airlines on Grandma Juliana's last trip back from Italy. Before she left Rome, she bought a two-foot-tall statue of St. Joseph of Cupertino, patron saint for air travelers. She insisted on havin' St. Joseph in the seat next to her for the flight home. The problem for the airline was, she didn't think she should have to pay for the extra seat and threatened the poor stewardess with "eternal damnation" if she tried to stash him in the overhead compartment. Grandma Juliana finally agreed to let him ride upright in the captain's closet, but only if she could have the seat closest to the cockpit, which of course was first class, though she had only paid for coach.

Anyway, Grandma Juliana promised me "a big surprise" if I could memorize the names of all of her saint statues, and there are *a lot* of them. I'm thinkin', maybe a horse, bicycle, trip to Italy …? It took me two weeks before I could recite them all back to her, and guess what I got? I'm lookin' at it. My St. Francis of Assisi, patron saint of animals, statue. She had him shipped to me the minute she heard about my critter cemetery. She calls it my "zoo," which is fine, but it's the only zoo I know of full of dead animals, being guarded by a statue of a dead saint, but … whatever.

Now, I don't know for sure if God has a special place for these animals in heaven, or if He's just plannin' to start all over with new ones, but I would be so happy to get to heaven and find all of these dead animals waitin' for me and thankin' me for caring about them. I will try and remember to give St. Francis some of the credit as well. I put my sign in the sun to dry, then head back to the cabin.

J. R. and Danny have become true fishin' mates. They spend every mornin' together out on that water. I wanted to tag along today, but J. R. says he finally has someone normal to hang out with, and isn't gonna turn a good fishing trip into a sissy trip. Then he says, "Hey, speaking of normal, Danny wants to know why you're the only one in our family with a Southern accent."

Now I want to curl up and die. "What'd you tell him?"

"The truth."

"Which is ...?"

"You're a nutcase."

"J. R., that's not funny, and it's not the truth. I'm just expandin' my foreign language capabilities, that's all."

"A. J., I hate to be the one to break this to you, but Southern is not considered a foreign language in this country."

I cover my head with my beach towel. How am I ever supposed to show my face again now that Danny knows I'm a fake? I may as well just stay under this towel the rest of my life.

"Ahh, don't fret, little sis. Danny Boy said he thought it was 'kinda cute' the way you tried to pull that off. Said that's a first to meet someone who actually wants to speak with a Southern accent. Most folks just like to make fun of it."

"Really? He said that?"

"Hey, it's nothing to be *proud* of, for Pete's sake. It just means you didn't make as big a fool of yourself as you could have."

I just fling that towel off my head and go skippin' on down to the dock with Mama and the twins. Danglin' my feet in the water, I start singin',

"... two drifters, off to see the world, there's such a lot of world to see. We're after the same rainbow's end, waitin' 'round the bend, my huckleberry friend, Sailor, and me...."

The twins just look at me, then over at Mama. "Don't look at me," Mama says. "I'm the last person on earth to know what's going on in that head of hers. But it must be something good."

7

Turnin' Ten
July 20, 1968

Today is my birthday. I'm turnin' ten. It's funny how on your birthday you never feel older than the day before. But if you look back a year, then you seem older, but you never feel the *gettin'* older.

Since I don't have any friends out here, I won't be havin' a real party, just a family party. This mornin' my brothers are helpin' me make a secret outdoor run for my hamster to play in. J. R.'s helpin' Dino and Benji hollow out some tree branches for Ruby to use as tunnels. That's what they're givin' me for my birthday present. Ruby Jean can only be outside when I'm with her—or she might dig herself out of the run and I'd never see her again.

I let my brothers in on my secret about Ruby because it's been killin' me to keep all that guilt to myself. They swear never to tell. They know if they do, I'll fink on 'em about the broken windows in the abandoned house back home. They play this game where they see how close they can come to not hittin' the windows with rocks. If you hit a window, you lose.

After breakfast, me and Sailor decide to visit Mr. Mueller. I want to give him a soap carving I've made for him. It's supposed to be a carving of my hamster, but it looks more like a rat with a fat nose. We're dawdlin' along in the woods, just smellin' the sweet pitchy pines, when guess who we see together? My sister and Danny's brother. Oh, surprise, surprise, they finally found each other. Adriana gave me a new diary for my birthday, which I will probably fill up just writin' about her and her new island beau.

I already filled up an entire diary the night Adriana went bowlin'. Back at our real home, Adriana asked Daddy if she could go bowlin' with a bunch of her school friends at Sally's Alley. Daddy let her go, but he told her she needed to be home by eleven or she'd be sorry. Well, at eleven thirty Daddy left the house with his hair slicked back with Vitalis and wearin' a set of fake buckteeth and his too-small ranger uniform that he keeps for special occasions like this. The best part was he let me come too in my pajamas—after he blacked out one of my big front teeth. So in we walked to Sally's and headed right for Adriana's big group of friends. Daddy says, in a perfect hillbilly accent, "Adrianer, you best git yer tail end on out ter the truck faster'n a jackrabbit. Yer maw is worr'd sumpin' fierce, and yer po baby sissy here cain't sleep 'er wink 'til you's home whur you belongs." It was the funniest night of my life, and Adriana's worst, but she hasn't been late ever since.

Me and Sailor spy on Adriana and Jason for a while, but it's just a lot of gettin'-to-know-ya chitchat. Then Sailor gets Adriana's scent and darts right over to her. I duck behind a big tree trunk and try and sneak away.

"Hey, A. J., just a wild guess that's you over there. Why don't you get lost—maybe you'll run into Falling Rock." Then she snickers with Island Boy about me believin' that story.

Idiots.

I'm more curious to see how Mr. Mueller's gettin' on with all of his Oklahoma kinfolk and their big fancy hen parties anyway. I find the old man out diggin' up potatoes from his potato hill. "Hey there, Mr. Mueller."

"Mornin'," is all he says back.

"Fine bunch 'a potatoes you got there."

"Humph," he grunts.

"Hey, did you know that t'day's my birthday? I'm turnin' ten."

"Happy birthday."

He doesn't sound like someone should sound when they're wishin' you a happy birthday. "You okay, Mr. Mueller?"

"Just tired's all. The ladies are talkin' of makin' some potato salad this afternoon. 'Course it probably never dawned on them that potatoes come from under the ground. Doubt if a one of 'em ever got their fingernails dirty diggin' one up."

That's when it hits me that diggin' up these potatoes might be makin' him think about his dead wife—the potato truck, and all. I just want to change the topic of potatoes real fast. "Are you enjoyin' all your Southern comp'ny, Mr. Mueller?"

"Lotta work keepin' 'em all happy. My youngest grandson seems to be the only considerate one in the bunch."

"How's that, Mr. Mueller?" Now he really has me curious.

"Well, the ladies all seem to think this is some darned luxury resort I'm runnin' out here. S'pectin' me to wait on 'em hand and foot. Danny's the only one ever askin' how he can help me or doin' for the others so I don't have to do so much."

"That's a fine grandson you got yourself there, Mr. Mueller. I can tell just by the way he acts and talks that he's the carin' type."

"Well, guess I'll be gettin' on back with these potatoes 'fore the ladies all come hollerin' for somethin' more."

"Oh, hey, I made somethin' for you." I take that rat-lookin' hamster out from my duffel bag and hand it to Mr. Mueller.

"Why, A. J.," he says kinda quiet, "that's real kind of you to make that for me."

"It's nothin'," I say, and give him a smile.

He walks away clutchin' that sack of potatoes in one hand and my rat hamster in the other. Then he turns around and looks back at me. "Happy birthday, A. J.," he says real nice this time. I swear I see him smile when he looks down at my soap carving in his hand. That's the first time I've seen him smile in a long while.

When Daddy comes home, he surprises me with my own pair of binoculars, which I have wanted for a very long time. Then Mama cooks me up my favorite dinner, cheeseburgers with homemade fries. And for dessert, we're gonna have hand-cranked fresh peach ice cream to go with my birthday cake. Adriana gets to dinner late because she was "just out for a walk." I give her a little smirk from across the table and get one of her death stares in return.

Everybody sings "Happy Birthday," and I blow out all of my candles—after makin' my wish—which I will not even mention or it will not come true. I open my birthday cards that Daddy picked up at our mailbox when he was in town today. I got five dollars from Grandma Angelina, and a money tree full of dimes from Grandma Juliana, totaling one dollar. Then I got a card from my best friend, Dorie, and one from my cousin Stacy, who just wants to let me know that she got a new car for her sixteenth birthday last week. She says it looks like our T-Bird, only hers is red and brand new. Her mama is my mama's sister, my Aunt Genevieve. Her daddy imports antiques from the Old Country and sells them here for a bundle. Mama says their family is very well-to-do. Daddy says they're just stinking rich and like to brag about it.

I read my card from Stacy out loud to Daddy.

"How about that," Daddy says, "a fancy *brand-new* T-Bird." He whistles. "Hey, you be sure and write back about your *brand-new* binoculars, A. J." He tosses his head back laughing. "And don't forget to tell her about the vinyl shoulder strap that goes with 'em."

I'd rather have my binoculars anyway. You can't see the heavens through the windshield of a car.

After dinner, I go to Juniper Beach with my binoculars to watch the stars come out. I always thank the Lord for holding all those stars in space so none of them drop down here and burn us all to smithereens. But I also tell Him how nice I think it is of Him to make such a pretty sky for us at night.

I sometimes get carried away tryin' to look through the galaxy to see how far it goes, but then that infinity thing starts up and I have to stop myself before I go absolutely berserk. I'm just startin' up with that kind of thinkin' when someone comes up behind me and scares the livin' daylights outta me.

"Hey, A. J." It's Danny. "Sorry I scared ya." He must've seen the look on my face and knew he'd spooked me. He comes and sits with us on the cool sand. Sailor sits between us. "What are you lookin' at up there?"

"Infinity," I say. "You ever think about how that sky just goes on and on forever and ever and never ends?"

"Only when I want to drive myself crazy." He grins.

"I just can't understand how infinity can never end. But if it did have an end, then what would be after that? And it's the same with heaven, and living forever and ever and ever. What on earth would we do up there for so long?"

Danny looks at me and laughs. "You sure have a big mind for someone your age, don't you?"

"I'm not that young anymore. I'm turnin' ten today. Didn't you ever wonder about infinity when you were ten?"

"I thought I was the only one who thought about things like that at your age, 'til I talked to my grandma about it."

"Your grandma? The one who died, you mean?" I was kind of afraid to ask, but I did.

"Yeah, she's the one who helped explain it all to me."

"How so?" I had to know.

"We were sittin' out on her porch swing one night, lookin' up at that sky, when I asked her the same thing you just asked. She said, 'Danny, God didn't give us minds to be able to understand everything. That's part of the mystery. Now, you can drive yourself crazy tryin' to understand somethin' you were never meant to figure out down here, or you can just trust Him 'til He's ready to let you in on it. 'Til then, just enjoy the mystery.'

"Then she told me, whenever I get scared about eternity, to just think of the most wonderful thing in the whole world, an' know heaven will be even better than that."

"So what do you think of?"

Danny looks at me with the most peaceful look I think I've ever seen on anybody. "The stars on a summer's night," he says, then looks up into that dark night sky.

After we find the Big Dipper, Danny says, "Hey, A. J., how would you like to see the stars from out on the water?"

"What? You mean swim out there?"

"No," he says laughing, "the rowboat." He points down the beach to the little dinghy pulled up onshore.

"You rowed here?"

"Sure did. So, what do you say?"

"S-sure, I've never looked at stars from a rowboat before."

Once we're all settled, with Sailor in his rightful place at the stern, me at the bow, and Danny in the middle, Danny asks, "Which way, A. J.?"

"Let's just drift."

So, we shove off with the oars, then lay them on the floorboards and "drift out to sea." When we're lookin' at the Little Dipper, Danny says, "My grandma once told me that stars are just tiny windows into heaven."

"You think your grandma's up there with Jesus right now?"

"I *know* that's where she is. I know it like I know my name."

"How do you know that for sure?" I ask.

"Some things you just feel in your soul, an' you know they're so."

We stay out driftin' forever, it seems, just listenin' to the silence. But in that silence, when I look up in that sky, I can hear the wonder of God louder than anything I've ever heard in all my life. Out on that dark lake, under those stars, somethin' big is goin' on. Somethin' big, and mysterious, and holy.

And that's where I turn ten.

8

Exposed

There is only one reason an entire family of seven would force themselves out of bed at the crack of dawn during the summer: Sunday-morning Mass. So, here we all are, piling out of our boat onto the main shore, and guess who pulls up alongside of us? The Oklahoma Fashion Squad from Bloomingdale's ... or so it seems, the way they all pour out onto the landing in their high heels, fancy hats, and shiny lipstick.

The Morgans have this old boat of Mr. Mueller's that looks like a miniature tugboat. And here we are with our pink boat, dressed like we're straight off the set of the *Mickey Mouse Club*. Someone needs to call a boat swap here.

I'm tryin' to hide behind Mama so no one can see where I spilled my orange juice down the front of my culottes. I turn my head back to watch Danny and Jason tie up the tug, when my mama pulls a fast one on me.

Sometimes I cannot believe that woman is my mother. She swoops on over to all those ladies and starts chattin' up a storm. The next thing I know, she's invited them all over after church for a potluck and challenged them to a bocce ball tournament.

What is this? The Catholics versus the Baptists? These Okies don't stand a chance playin' bocce ball against a bunch of Italians. For Pete's sake—they probably don't even have a clue what bocce ball is.

Turns out, they'd be *"delight'd"* to come. Then off they go, tippy-toein' down the block to the Baptist church, right across the street from the Catholic church. Danny looks back and gives us a friendly nod. I wonder if there is anybody in the South who is not a Baptist. Don't believe I've ever heard of a Southern Catholic before.

Our church service was better than usual today. Hardly anybody was lookin' out the windows. The priest read from Psalm 19. The strangest thing, it sounded just like what was in my head that night I was lookin' up at the stars and hearin' the wonder of God:

> The heavens declare the glory of God; and the firmament sheweth his handywork.
>
> Day unto day uttereth speech, and night unto night sheweth knowledge.
>
> There is no speech nor language, where their voice is not heard.
>
> Their line is gone out through all the

> earth, and their words to the end of the world.

Boy, don't I know it.

After returnin' home from church, I find Mama in the kitchen cookin' up her favorite Italian dish, gnocchi, for the potluck. She just loves these little potato dumplins all smothered in sauce. She's singin' "O Sole Mio," while she's boilin' up the pasta.

"What time is this shindig s'posed to start, Mama?"

"Around three o'clock. You're planning to play bocce, aren't you?"

"Maybe." *I'm not real sure I want to take advantage of these nice folks.*

"Of course you are. These are your kind of people, kiddo. You speak their language."

Maybe, but it's not very nice to whip the tar out of a bunch of Southerners who've never played bocce ball. I'm just not sure this is good sportsmanship.

"Hey, why don't you go help your dad set up for the tournament?"

I'd rather play with my hamster, but I decide to go see if he wants any help. Bocce ball is an Italian lawn bowling game that Daddy grew up on. We have this dirt court all cleared out with sideboards for all the boundaries. There's this little ball called the boccino, and the object is to get as many of your team's balls as close to the boccino as you can. It takes years of practice to learn how to either roll your ball right up to that boccino or knock the other team's ball away from it. I just hate the thought of humiliatin' our comp'ny.

Three o'clock sharp, our competitors show up with armloads of food. Bowls filled to the brim with potato salad, Jell-O heaped with whipped cream, and fried chicken that makes my mouth water just lookin' at it. Once all the food's set out, I know which end of the table I'm sittin' at. We all gather around, and Daddy leads us in grace. Jason grabs a seat right next to Adriana. Daddy ends up at the head by Mama. By the time Danny sits down, the only seat left is at the foot, catty-corner from me.

J. R.'s on the other side of Danny, so they start right up talkin' about fishin'. That gives me the freedom to devour my potato salad and chicken without givin' manners a second thought. I stop just short of lickin' my fingers. Soon as I ask Danny to "please pass the Jell-O," he starts talkin' to me.

"Hey, found any star constellations yet with your new binoculars?" He talks to me like a real nice big brother would talk, not like mine talks to me.

"Nope. Don't really look for the constellations much." *Please don't ask me why.*

"Why's that?"

"Umm," *sigh.* "Okay … last summer our Bluebird troop went on a weekend campout. We were all sleepin' by the river under a sky full of stars, when Mandi Klowski started talkin' about the Zodiac Killer. She said he follows the constellations, and whoever he finds sleepin' right under the signs of the zodiac, he chops 'em all to bits.

"Well, bein' that I was only a Bluebird, I wanted to go home. Instead, I was stuck out on this sandbar, sure that I was layin' directly beneath those zodiac signs. Everyone else fell right to sleep, and there I was, jumpy as a baby jackrabbit, just waitin' to get chopped up. All of a sudden, someone flung their arm across me in their sleep. I have *never* screamed so loud in my whole life. Woke up the entire Bluebird troop, as well as all the leaders. No one was very nice to me after that.

"So, the next day, I came home from camp and quit the Bluebirds. Mama told the Bluebird leaders that if she had wanted her eight-year-old daughter to hear stories like that, she would have sent me to Jack the Ripper Camp. She said she had expected something more from the Bluebirds of America and that they had better cut the killer stories before a lot more kids quit.

"That's why I don't like to look for the constellations. Just bad memories, I guess."

Danny gives me an understanding nod. "Yeah, I can see what you mean. You should look for the Bear constellation sometime though; he's not a part of the zodiac."

"That's a relief."

Danny looks around the table, then leans over and whispers. "Looks like Jason and your sister have disappeared."

He's right. Everyone else seems to be talkin' back 'n forth, but there is no Jason or Adriana anywhere in sight. "Oh brother, here she goes again."

"Here she goes again … in what way?" Danny wants to know.

"Here she goes fallin' in love again."

"Man, I hope not."

"Why not?" I ask.

"Because Jason already has a girl back home, and he'd better not be leadin' your sister on."

"Would he *do that?*"

"Sorry to say, he probably would, and it wouldn't be the first time." Danny has a sad, faraway look in his eyes. Then, as if talking to himself, he adds, "Like father, like son."

My daddy gets up and announces the teams for bocce ball. To my surprise, he mixes us Italians in with the Okies, probably to give them a fightin' chance. I feel good about that. My team has Danny, his mama, Aunt Charlotte, and me. Daddy's team has Mama, J. R., Aunt Rebecca, and himself. No one under ten is allowed to play because of the weight of the balls, just in case they drop one on their toes. The twins get to keep score, and everyone else just wants to watch anyway.

Danny goes first. Darned if he doesn't land his ball right next to that boccino. "How'd you do that your first time?" I ask him.

He looks over at me and smiles. "Bocce ball ain't a whole lot different from horseshoes."

Of course. I realize right then that these Okies might be more of a match than I thought they'd be. By the end of the second game we're one and one. We all decide to go game three for the Grand Championship or, as Danny calls it, the Rubber Match.

We weren't doin' so hot at first, due to Aunt Charlotte's goofy aimin'. But thanks to Danny, we're right back on top by the final play of the game. It's my turn to make the winning score. Here we are, all three of our balls positioned for points. This is like bases loaded in baseball. If I can get my ball to knock out their one solid, I can win this game with honors for my team. It will be like a grand slam.

I'm all charged up like I'm in the World Series. I line myself up and eye that little boccino 'til I have it etched in my mind. I close my eyes for a split second and play it all through in my head. Then I swing my arm back and hurl that ball like I'm pitchin' for the New York Yankees.

I watch my ball hit the other ball all right. *The wrong ball.* It hits the boccino and knocks it clear out of range from our other three stripes, then butts it right up to their cluster of solids.

"Done like a true Italian," J. R. announces to the crowd.

"No." I cry. *This can't be.* I'm horrified. I lost the game for my team. We lost the Grand Championship. We lost the Rubber Match. *How can I face Danny? How can I face any of them? I can't.* I take off running.

I head for the woods like I'm runnin' for my life. I run 'til I can't breathe anymore, 'til I just fall on my knees at the edge of my cemetery. I want to dig a hole in the ground and bury myself next to everything else I've buried there. Then I hear a rustlin' comin' from the clearing where all of my animals are laid to rest. I brush back a tree bough....

"Get ouuut!" I scream. "Get away from my animals. You're stepping on them—*all over them."* I'm shakin' like a crazy person. "How dare you *kiss* in *my* cemetery." I'm

shovin' and pushin' them. They're tramplin' my sacred buried animals.

Jason tries to stop me. "Hey, settle down, kid." He tries to take me by my shoulders.

"You ..." I glare at him. I can barely get my words out. "You ... *jerk.* You leave my sister alone. You don't love her ... now get OUT."

Jason walks out of my cemetery, then turns and waits.

"Stop it, A. J.," Adriana yells at me.

"And you ... he doesn't love you. You let them all kiss you ... *Why?"* I sob.

Adriana sneers at me. "You say anything about this, A. J., and Mom and Dad will hear all about your stinky little rodent hiding in the shed." Then she turns and walks away with *him*, leaving me all alone.

I lie down on the ground, right there by my dead animals, and cry. I cry about makin' a fool of myself at bocce ball. I cry for my sister and for believing it should all mean more. And, I cry that I'm not nine years old anymore. The best year of my life is over.

9

Mama's Pink Villa

My Aunt Genevieve called Mama to try and arrange a family reunion in Tuscany at some ancient villa in the middle of a grape field. Mama told her that it wasn't in a park ranger's salary for a family of seven to tootle off to Italy to frolic through a vineyard. Daddy told Mama that he didn't need to travel halfway around the world to be tortured by more of her relatives, when he got all he needed right here with Grandma Juliana. But he warned Mama never to invite them to our island either. He said the last thing he needed was to be the brunt of all of Uncle Nick's jokes in his only place of refuge. The last time we went to their house, for Uncle Nick's mandatory fortieth surprise party, he introduced Daddy to all of their friends as the Indian Lake *Trailer Park Ranger*, instead of *State Park Ranger*.

Daddy told Uncle Nick that he has a few friends in the Mafia he'd like to introduce him to, if he keeps introducing him that way.

Another thing that drives Daddy crazy is listenin' to Uncle Nick say, "There's nothing money can't buy." Daddy says he can think of two things it hasn't bought Uncle Nick and Aunt Genevieve: class and tactfulness, and in Uncle Nick's case, it would be nice if it could just buy a muzzle.

The tough part for Daddy is that Uncle Nick is ... well, *family*. When Uncle Nick married Mama's sister, he was instantly propelled into "The Family Dynasty," which connects you for life to everyone else in The Dynasty. It also commits you to a whole set of rules and obligations that only Mama's family knows about. That's why when Mama says we are spendin' a weekend with the Sophronia cousins, you just nod and pack your bags. It's not a suggestion open for discussion. And that's how Mama got Daddy to agree to hook up with the cousins for a weekend at the Potholes in Eastern Washington. There's somethin' mandatory in The Dynasty Rule Book about seein' your relatives at least once a year, and our time for this year is up.

Daddy loved to go to the Potholes as a boy, so Mama figured she could at least offer that as a consolation prize for him havin' to go along with the plan. And *that's* where we're headin' for the weekend, so Mama can see her sister, while the rest of us "serve our time," as Daddy puts it.

Daddy says the Potholes are these gigantic sand dunes that rise up out of the reservoir, like little sand islands. Each mornin', you launch your boat out on the reservoir and make a mad dash to pick out your own island for the day. Once you stake your umbrella in the sand, it's like sayin',

"This is our island; go find your own." Usually, you get the island all to yourself, but sometimes, if you find a big island, you might end up with only half of it. After you've marked your territory, you unload your boatload of food and coolers, then you go water-skiin', swimmin', and inner-tubin' 'til the sun goes down. Then you pull your boat back to the motel and launch it again the next day.

This mornin' I snuck out to the shed and loaded Ruby up with a weekend's supply of food and a peanut butter cracker. She wasn't real happy about gettin' woke up when she had just gone to bed for the day. She looked awful—like my Grandma Juliana looks in the mornin' when her eyes are all squinty. She must've had quite a night last night. I wish I could clock her wheel for mileage; I have a feelin' she runs about five miles at a sprint. I'd hate to get woke up after a night like that too, but it was the only time I could say good-bye before appearin' for duty on the dock at o-seven-hundred to help load everything into the boat. If you're late for that, you automatically get stuck with the worst seat in the car for the trip.

At exactly o-seven-hundred sharp, Daddy had us all line up in an assembly line to toss in the inner tubes, skis, fishin' poles, coolers, tons of pop, chips, beach towels, you name it, *everything* went in the boat except us kids and the dog. Actually, we went in too, until we got to the mainland. Then we hooked the boat up to the hitch and piled into the station wagon for the long, hot road trip to Eastern Washington. We drew straws to see who'd get the front seat with Mama and Daddy, the window seats, and the way back with Sailor. The loser got stuck in the middle of everybody else. Guess who lost? Thank you very much.

We started out pretty happy, but once we were on the road for about an hour, we'd all had enough of Twenty Questions, *and* counting peanut cars, *and* findin' the letters of the alphabet in all the road signs and license plates. That was just about the time Dino decided to asked the forbidden question: "Are we there yet?" It's things like this I look forward to most, if for no other reason than it helps to break up the monotony, and you never know what's gonna happen, because no one has had the guts, until now, to ask that question.

Once the words spill out of Dino's mouth, Daddy pulls right over on the side of the road. He warned us from the get-go that if we started to whine, fight, or ask, "Are we there yet?" he would pull over and put us all in the boat for the duration of the trip. I am so excited because I would really love to ride in the boat, especially if Dino's the one who gets in trouble for askin' and not me.

Daddy turns around and looks right at Dino. "Dino, I'm not sure I heard you correctly. Is there a problem?"

Dino looks around, and I'm nodding, tryin' to hint to him to go ahead and say it again. But Dino backs down. "No—I'm fine."

"That's what I thought you said." Then he pulls back onto the highway.

Rats. There goes my only chance to ride in the boat. This is gonna be the longest, hottest drive, especially when I'm crammed between two other kids, with a big hairy dog droolin' down my back. Even when you roll all the windows down for fresh air, the air outside is hotter than the air inside. It's so blazin' hot, you can even see mirages on the road ahead.

Suddenly, we spot the A&W and beg Daddy to stop for some ice-cold root beer, but he tries to tell us it's only a mirage.

"No it's not," we're all yellin' back.

"Yeah, it is, but if you insist on drinking imaginary root beer, that's fine with me." Then he swerves off the highway into the A&W parking lot.

Root beer never tastes so good as when you are dyin' of thirst and you slug down a big ice-cold mug of it. We buy an extra jug to take with us too. As soon as we're back on the road, Benji starts to whine about needin' to go to the bathroom, so Daddy pulls off the highway and tells him to go right there on the side of the road.

"I'm not peeing in front of everyone," Benji yells back.

Daddy rolls his eyes and tries to explain to him that that's what men do when they're out in the middle of nowhere.

"Well, I'm not a man, and I'm not peeing out there."

"Just go stand behind a tumbleweed then," Daddy says back.

"What if there's a rattlesnake—he'll jump out and bite me."

By now everyone else is startin' to need to go too just thinkin' about it so much.

J. R. says he will go with Benji if Benji will promise to go. Then Dino says he'll go too. So finally, Benji agrees and climbs out of the car. I just about die laughin' when I see all three of my brothers peein' together along the side of the road. Mama decides this would make for a fine Polaroid memory and leans out of the car window to snap a shot of their little behinds all lined up, side by side. We have got to be the weirdest family on earth.

Once we see the turnoff to the Lakeview Motel, Daddy tells Mama that it's just a mirage too, and he speeds right past it.

"Sonny Degulio, you'd better turn this car around right now," Mama warns him.

Daddy looks at Mama. "Do I have to?"

Mama glares back. "Yes, you do."

After a good loud groan, Daddy makes a big U-turn and takes us back, sayin' that of all the mirages, he wished this one were the real thing, and he still hoped it would all disappear when we got there. Mama's relatives are *not* my daddy's favorite people to spend his vacation time with. But Daddy loves the Lakeview Motel, and he loves Mama even more, which is why he agreed to go.

The Lakeview Motel is where Daddy always stayed for his family vacations in the olden days. It's a *historical* pink brick lodge that sits on a small pond, with a dock and two rowboats. When we pull up to the lobby, Daddy looks at Mama and says, "Well, what do you think?" Mama steps out of the car and looks around. "Where's the lake?"

Daddy climbs out of the car too and goes to stand by Mama. He puts his arm around her and says, "Sophie, that's the special thing about the Lakeview Motel—there is no lake. It's for people with big imaginations. But, there is this nice little pond stocked full of fish. And if you crane your neck as far as you can to your right, from the upstairs window, you can see the reservoir from there."

As soon as the twins hear the word *fish*, they start pullin' all of their fishin' gear out of the boat as fast as they can. "I got dibs on the new pole," Benji yells.

"It won't matter what pole you have, you never catch anything anyway," Dino yells back and grabs "Old Faithful," Daddy's old pole.

Daddy has told them that even the worst fisherman in the whole world could catch a fish at the Lakeview trout pond. "Dino, be sure and watch your hook, and keep it out of Benji's back this time, okay, buddy?"

"Okay, Dad," Dino calls back, as he runs for the pond with his loose fishhook swinging wildly in all directions.

Me and Daddy are walkin' toward the lobby to get our room key, when the cousins roll in, pullin' their sparklin' blue jet boat behind their matchin' blue pickup truck. It looks like someone dumped a truckload of glitter all over the top of their boat.

I look over at Daddy, who has stopped dead in his tracks. He looks back at Mama and shields his eyes as though he's goin' blind just from starin' at it and says, "Hey-ho, the gang's all here."

My uncle Nick is a big hairy Greek with a loud voice. The family scandal on Uncle Nick is, Grandma Juliana thinks he's Italian. Aunt Genevieve met him and fell in love with him while traveling abroad, *then* realized there was no way Grandma Juliana would put up with one of her daughters marryin' beneath their Italian lineage. Especially a

Greek. But, being that Nick was dark and obnoxiously loud, she never questioned that he wasn't Italian. Even his name was close enough that Grandma Juliana didn't suspect anything. The real nightmare came when Grandma Juliana insisted on meeting Nick's family, who would never in their life pretend to be Italians and would be completely insulted by the whole notion that Italians are better than Greeks. That left Genevieve and Nick no choice but to elope, since both families were planning to attend the wedding. Everyone was really mad that they weren't included in the nuptials, but little did they know the real disaster that would have gone down in The Dynasty Diaries had they gone through with their original plan.

So far they've been able to ward off the Sophronia-Juliana get-together for eighteen years. But I'm prayin' that it all comes to a head when Grandma Juliana and the Sophronias all end up in Italy together this fall. That is one family reunion I would give my right arm to attend.

Uncle Nick hops down from his pickup truck, looks over at our boat, and laughs. "Hey, Sonny, why don't you trade in that piece of pink driftwood for something like this baby?" Then he struts over to Daddy and gives him a big bear hug.

"How's it going, N-ick?" Daddy tries to say, while he's gettin' the air squeezed out of him.

Aunt Genevieve runs over to Mama in her spiky high heels and twirls around like she's showin' off how good she looks in her too-tight pedal pushers. "Can you tell I've lost weight?" she says, and gives Mama a hug and a kiss. I'm thinkin' that if she turned around she'd probably find it, 'cause it looks like it got shifted around to her backside.

Once she spots me, I try and hide behind Daddy. She's that huggy-kissy type, and she's comin' straight at me with her bright red lips that will end up all over my face once she gets ahold of me.

The two cousins, Stacy and Nicky Jr., hop down from the truck and just stand there staring at the motel like there's somethin' wrong with it. "We aren't really staying here, are we?" Stacy whines.

"I hope not," Nicky echoes, equally as whiney. "This place is a dive."

We haven't seen our cousins for a real long time, but they act like we aren't even here. All they seem to care about is not stayin' at our motel.

Big Nick takes a look around. "I've heard of roughin' it, Sonny, but you gotta be kidding, right?"

Daddy doesn't even bother to answer. He calls Uncle Nick and Nicky Jr. "Hercules and Zeus" when they aren't around. Uncle Nick acts like a big hotshot, and Nicky Jr. tries to act just like him, but he's just a scrawny little thirteen-year-old with a big mouth.

"How 'bout we all stay at one of the newer hotels on the reservoir—our treat, really—nothin' money can't buy." Uncle Nick's struttin' around like a peacock showin' off his feathers.

Aunt Genevieve looks at Mama. "Oh, do come with us, Soph. We just drove past a real classy place right on the water, with a huge pool for the kids. Who wants to swim in a pond with fish, anyway?"

I can see the veins in Daddy's neck poundin' away, but all he says is, "Well, Nick, my family enjoys the rustic setting and fish pond, but you're more than welcome to stay at a place more suitable for your family."

Aunt Gen looks at Mama like she feels sorry for her havin' to stay here. "We'll book the penthouse and have you all over to see pictures of the Tuscan villa we're rebuilding for our second home."

"Rebuilding?" Daddy asks. "Why, I thought folks like you would want to buy a new villa."

Uncle Nick belts out a laugh. "That's funny, Sonny, a *new* villa. I think the newest villas in Italy are about a hundred years old. But this one will look better than new by the time we're finished, trust me. The neighbors will wonder who in the world would paint their villa blue, but it's kind of our signature color, if you know what I mean."

"Yep, I know exactly what you mean, Nick. Pink is our signature color, so we'll be happy staying right here with our pink boat and pink motel—but, by all means, I insist you take your family up the road where the rest of the classy folks are staying."

I could tell what Daddy was really thinkin', but they just thought he was bein' polite to offer them a better place.

"Well, if you're sure." Uncle Nick signals to his family to hop back in the truck. The cousins look at us like we're weird for stayin' here.

"We'll give you a call to make dinner plans once we've checked in," Aunt Gen announces while climbing back into the cab. "Any good suggestions?"

Daddy cuts in before Mama has a chance to answer. "Actually, we've got reservations over at Dick's Drive-In when we're done fishing."

"Ha." Uncle Nick snorts. "Reservations at Dick's. Too funny, Sonny—hey, that rhymes."

Daddy glances over at Mama and rolls his eyes. Then he turns back toward Uncle Nick and says, "I think we'll just turn in early tonight and plan to meet up with you all in the morning at the reservoir."

We all wave as they roll back out onto the highway. Daddy and Mama both let out a big sigh. Daddy looks at the motel. "Well, it ain't Italy, baby, but welcome to your pink villa."

Mama leans over and kisses Daddy on the cheek. "I'll take you and my pink villa over Nick and a blue villa in Italy any day." Then she looks it over and calls it *Villa Rosa Mia*, meaning "My Pink Villa."

That makes Daddy smile.

Me and J. R. run to our motel room to get dibs on our beds. Our room has its own kitchenette, two big beds, a set of bunks, and a foldout couch. My bed even has a machine that takes coins and makes it vibrate. Adriana comes in long enough to change into her bathing suit, then heads to the pond. J. R. decides to go fishin' and follows her out.

I feel like explorin' with Sailor, who has to be tied up when I'm not playin' with him. We take a short trail and find a gift shop where they sell ice cream cones and candy. There are no dogs allowed inside, so I tell Sailor to stay while I pop in to check out the candy supply. He's pretty good about stayin' until he spots a few squirrels and goes tearin' after them with his leash draggin' behind him. After he trees the squirrels, he finally comes back. He gets no candy from me for runnin' off like that, and he knows why. After I eat all four pieces of saltwater taffy, slowly, in front of him, we head back to the pond where the rest of my family is hangin' out.

The twins and J. R. are fishin' away on the dock, while Adriana is all set up on her little beach mat, workin' away on that tan of hers again. Me and Sailor find a nice spot of shade under a weepin' willow tree, where we lie on our backs and look up at the clouds. Sailor is the only dog I know who plays dead without being told to. He just likes to lie on his back for no good reason.

At first, I'm all happy and peaceful just watchin' the clouds go by. But then, the clouds start to look like cotton candy, which reminds me of the time Cousin Stacy ate so much cotton candy at the fair that she threw up on the merry-go-round. I was the lucky one on the horse right next to hers—the one that went down when hers went up—which is the worst possible place to be when someone is throwing up. That makes me think about my cousins and how they're up the road at some fancy hotel—with a big pool that probably has a slide *and* a diving board—and all of a sudden somethin' just doesn't seem fair here.

Mama and Daddy are sittin' together at the end of the dock with their feet in the water, drinkin' root beer over ice. I go out there to throw a stick for Sailor off the dock, but instead I end up sayin' somethin' stupid. "How come we have to stay here instead of at a nice place with the cousins?"

Daddy looks at me. "Excuse me?"

I know I should just say "never mind," but it doesn't come out that way. Instead it comes out as, "This place is dumb—I want to go swimmin' in a nice big swimmin' pool without stinky fish in it."

My mama's head jerks around real fast, which is always a bad sign. She looks right at me with those raised eyebrows she gets when you've said the wrong thing and says, "Well, well ... who shoved a silver spoon in your mouth when you were born?"

I don't remember anyone ever shovin' a silver spoon in my mouth, only a plastic one. Mama used to feed the twins and me in the bathtub when we were little. She just brought in a little dinner tray of food and a spoon and shoveled the stuff into our mouths while we played in the tub. She didn't see the point in messin' with three bibs and three high chairs, when she could just feed us in the tub and wash it all down the drain when we were done.

"Nobody," I answered back. "But it doesn't seem fair that they get to have everything so nice, and we don't."

Daddy told me to come sit down next to him. Sailor came and sat on my other side. "A. J., I want you to take a good look around and tell me what you see."

"Well, I see a pond, some trees, a pink motel, and some rollin' hills."

Then Daddy says, "Can I tell you what I see?"

"Yeah." *As long as you don't say you see a spoiled rotten kid who'd better zip it before she gets her mouth washed out with soap.*

"I look around, and I see my boys fishing on a pond full of trout, and I remember being a boy here myself. I see my oldest daughter lying in the sun, listening to music. I've been watching my youngest daughter and her dog, beneath a shady tree, watching the clouds go by. I'm sitting by the most beautiful woman in the world, wondering how a guy like me ever got this lucky. And all I am thinking inside is, *Thank You, God, for life is good.*"

10

Sand and Surf

"Good morning, campers...." Daddy jolts us out of a dead sleep with his park ranger megaphone. Once I remember where I am, I realize I must've passed out on the vibrating bed last night and slept like a baby 'til that blaring speaker scared me outta my wits. Adriana awakes all grumpy from havin' to share a bed with me. She says she got no sleep at all 'cause I was thrashing around so much. I tell her to cheer up, that she has all day ahead to spend with Cousin Stacy. Adriana and Cousin Stacy are the same age, but Adriana has a hard time listenin' to her brag about how popular she is and how she's goin' steady with the most popular boy at her school. Everyone knows that any girl going steady is given a St. Christopher necklace—even if they aren't Catholic. So, last time we saw her, Adriana asked to see proof of her St. Christopher, and Stacy told her she left it at home because it was solid gold and she didn't want anything to happen to it. We never believe a word she says.

Mama's in the kitchenette fryin' up the twin's mornin' catch. I'm tryin' not to think about them sizzlin' away on the stove, after gettin' yanked out of the water by a big sharp hook. Poor fish. Talk about a lousy day. I'm stickin' to cold cereal myself. Whenever we travel, we get to have these miniature cereal boxes all to ourselves. You just punch 'em open, pour on the milk, and eat right out of the box. While I'm right in the middle of eatin' my Cocoa Crunchies, Daddy's voice comes blarin' through the speaker again, makin' me drop my spoon.

"Attention, campers. As soon as you're done eating, you all need to get into your bathing suits, use the bathroom—especially Benji—and get into the car … repeat; bathing suits, bathroom, car. Over and out."

Nothing like havin' a park ranger for a wake-up caller when you're on vacation.

On my way out to the car, I almost get run over by a young Mexican girl pushin' a cartful of towels and sheets. Her cart is piled so high that she couldn't see me.

"*Lo siento* … s-orry," she says, lookin' embarrassed. She's helpin' to make up the rooms with her mom and another girl who looks like her sister. Boy, they start workin' young around here.

I smile and say, "That's okay." Then I remember something I learned in Spanish from Señora Habara on TV in second grade. *"No problema,"* I add.

She smiles back. Once I'm in the car, I watch her from my window and start feelin' bad about what I said yesterday to Daddy. Here I am ready to go spend a day lying around in the sand and havin' fun on the water, and this girl and her family have to spend the day makin' beds and cleanin' up after people like us. I feel really sad that they're too poor to go play like other kids their age. Just as we're pullin' away, the girl looks right at me. That makes me feel even worse, like maybe I should just stay here and make my own bed. Instead I wave good-bye.

When we get to the boat launch, we don't see our cousins anywhere in the lineup for the launch. "It can't be too hard to find them—just look for the blinding blue boat," Daddy says. "I'm sure it's one of a kind."

"There it is," Dino yells. "It's already out on the water."

And there's my uncle Nick sittin' up on the back of the driver's seat, wearin' tiny black swim bottoms that look very small on his big hairy body. He looks like a gorilla in Jockey shorts.

"Oh please, spare me," my mom whispers to my dad, but I hear it anyway.

"Sonny," Uncle Nick yells, loud enough that everyone else looks too. "You're really thinkin' of launching *that*, when you can all ride in *My Big Fat Baby?*"

"They *didn't* name it …" Daddy mumbles, as his eyes dart to the words neatly aligned across the side of their boat in metallic silver letters.

They did.

"Hard to turn down ridin' in this baby when you have the same first name as the guy who wrote the song—Sonny Hall, '58."

"Just thought it would be nice to have a backup in case one of your jets goes out," Daddy yells back and laughs. Then he says to Mama, “I like to know I have a get-away boat in case I need one.”

Once we’re launched, we taxi over alongside of their boat. Our boat is loaded up with old wooden skis, patched-up truck inner tubes, and our plastic cooler. Theirs is loaded up with new competition water skis, store-bought inner tubes, and a shiny metal cooler. Stacy and Nicky are wearin’ Olympic bathing suits, but one is too chubby and the other is too wimpy to look like true Olympic swimmers. They still aren’t smiling. Nicky looks at our old skis. “You’re still skiing on those splinters?”

“Splinters,” Big Nick roars. “That’s funny—got your Old Man’s sense of humor, don’t ya, Son?”

J. R. looks at me like we need to come up with something good to deal with Nicky. We’re pretty creative when it comes to scheming up plans for hotshot thirteen-year-olds.

“Just lead us to an island,” Daddy yells over the sound of their loud jet engine.

So Uncle Nick takes off, full speed ahead, not realizing that the reason everyone else is goin’ so slow is because everyone else knows that if you’re not careful, you’re likely to run across a sandbar.

Sure enough, we all watch as the blue blaze jerks to a halt up ahead. We can hear the engine sputtering sand, as well as Uncle Nick sputtering cuss words all over the place. At least it gives us time to catch up to them. Daddy helps Uncle Nick get the boat off the sandbar and back on the water before all the good islands are taken. Of course Uncle Nick blames the sandbar for being there.

We finally beach our boats on a nice little island and stake our umbrellas in the sand. Me and Sailor are the first ones into the water for a swim. The water really is as warm as Daddy said it would be. When the reservoir laps up all around that hot sand, it heats the water right up. You can swim really far out, and it's still nice and shallow. I can still touch bottom, but Sailor can't, so we can't stay out here too long.

When we're swimmin' back toward shore, I pretend that me and Sailor got shipwrecked and are about to wash up on this deserted island. First we see some bright-colored umbrellas and beach blankets; then we see a big bright blue boat. Instead of it belongin' to a bunch of rude relatives who like to make fun of our family, I pretend that it belongs to the Cartwrights, and I'm about to be rescued by Little Joe. It's not long before my daydream is shattered by seeing Nicky struttin' down the beach in his skimpy little bathing suit.

Uncle Nick is revving up the jets and yellin' for anyone who wants to go skiing or tubing to get ready. J. R. says he'd like to go and is looking over their new ski like maybe he'd like to try it out. Then Nicky comes over and says, "That's *my* ski … and that's *our* boat, so it looks like I'm going first."

The day has only begun, but my daddy looks like he's already had enough. "J. R., go get your ski. I'll take you."

So J. R. grabs his own ski while Daddy starts up the *African Queen*. Me and Sailor volunteer to go along as spotters. We wait for Nicky to take off, but he falls four times in a row, and his dad finally tosses him a second ski and tells him he's not ready for one ski yet. Now we know the truth. So finally Nicky gets up on two skis and moves out of our way.

J. R. pops right up on one ski and heads out around the island. It's the funniest thing to see Nick Jr. goin' slower than molasses behind their jet boat, on two competition skis, while J. R. is skimmin' along behind our "pink driftwood," cuttin' back and forth, jumpin' the wake on his old "splinter."

J. R. is on his second lap around the island when we pass their jet boat. Nicky must've gotten tired and is tryin' to pull his scrawny body into the boat. I have this feelin' that it's all too tempting for J. R. to just ski right by, and I can see it comin'. J. R. jumps the wake and heads straight toward their boat, then makes a perfect cut, drenching 'em with spray. Me and Daddy just look at each other and smile. Daddy's right—*Life is good.*

When we get back to the island, Mama and Aunt Gen are sittin' with their lounge chairs halfway in the water, lookin' like a couple of Italian goddesses in big sun hats and Hollywood shades. I can see my Aunt Genevieve's hands wavin' wildly through the air and figure she's the one doin' most of the talkin'. I'm pretty sure she is the only woman alive who can outtalk my mama. Along with her talkin' hands, I can hear her "yack-yack-yack, blah-blah-blah" all the way across the water.

My mama likes her sister, but only in small doses. When they were growin' up, her sister always had to be The Queen, and Mama always got stuck being The Princess. But now that Mama's become The Queen of our family, she doesn't like to give up her throne very often.

Me and Sailor take a trek over the top of the sand dune to try and find Adriana and Stacy. Anytime you decide to go over the dune, you gotta bring a pop can full of water to pour on your feet along the way because the sand is so hot it will burn your feet. When we get to the top, we can see the twins fishin' from inner tubes in a little cove on the other side. Then we spot Adriana and Stacy lyin' on beach towels. They are doused in so much suntan oil that they look like a couple of greased pigs—Stacy looks like a fat greased pig, and Adriana looks like a skinny greased pig.

Cousin Stacy would be really pretty if she lost about fifty pounds. I remember when we were little, I used to think that Stacy stole all of little Nicky's food, and that's why she was so fat and he was so skinny. I told my mama that he was going to starve to death if she didn't stop it. I remember Mama tellin' me that boys can always eat more than girls and still be skinnier, but in heaven that all changes the other way around.

Although I don't like lying, I'm dyin' to get some of Stacy's big fib stories for my travel diary. I have a fiction section designated just for her. Once we get near their territory, me and Sailor sneak as close as we can and hide around the other side of their sandbank. I can barely make out anything Adriana is sayin', but I can hear Stacy loud and clear, just like Aunt Gen.

"... So, anyway, I got asked to our school prom by two different guys, the two most popular boys at our school, and I couldn't decide who to go with, but since I was already goin' steady with Bill, the quarterback, I just went with him. The other one was pretty jealous, but I danced with him, too, once we got there. He really wanted me to break up with Bill and go steady with him, but I didn't want to hurt Bill like that. Did you notice the St. Christopher Bill gave me?"

"That one's silver. I thought you said Bill gave you a solid gold one," Adriana says back.

"I did. I mean—he actually gave me two—this one and the gold one, but I only wear the gold one for special occasions because I don't like to get sand all over it."

There's this long silent pause. Then Adriana says, "Have you ever heard of a girl named Rachel Perry?"

"Yeah, she goes to my school. She's really popular, too. We're almost best friends."

"Yeah? Well, she's a really good friend of mine, too. We met at Bonnie Bell's Charm School. You know, I talked to her a few days ago and asked if she knew if you were still going steady with Bill, and she said she really doubted it because she and Bill have been together for over a year. Besides that, there's no way he could have danced with you because for one thing, he took Rachel, and for another, he had his leg in a cast from knee surgery and wasn't dancing with anyone at the prom."

It gets really quiet again, then suddenly Stacy blurts out, "Oh, my gosh—not *that* Bill." Then she laughs all nervous-like. "I didn't mean *Bill*, like Rachel's Bill. I meant a different Bill who's kind of new at our school. Rachel probably doesn't know him."

Oh brother … Give it up, Stacy.

Adriana says, "Umm, I'm going swimming."

All of a sudden she sticks her head around the side of

the sandbank. "I knew it," she says. "I can smell that wet dog anywhere." Then she whispers, "I hope you enjoyed the big whopper."

We both smile, and I have to cover my mouth so I don't start laughin'. Then Adriana turns and walks gracefully toward the water. Sometimes I actually like my sister.

11

Blessed Are the Poor

The sun is just startin' to go down when we return to our motel with another nutritious meal of Dick's burgers, shakes, and fries. Uncle Nick had tried to talk Daddy into havin' us join their family for seafood at Something's Fishy, but Daddy told him that the kids had waited all year to eat at Dick's Drive-In, and he just couldn't let us down on our last night of vacation. Mama pretty much lets Daddy call the shots about things like this. Usually by the time Daddy's had enough of Uncle Nick, we've had enough of the cousins, and Mama's had enough of her sister, too.

It's still nice and warm out, so we just unload all the food onto the picnic table by the pond. Just when I start to devour my hamburger, I notice the Mexican girl and her family sittin' on the dock eatin' tamales. I really want to meet her, so I take my fries and wander down to the dock like I'm just goin' there to look at the water. She smiles when she sees me so I wave and say, *"Hola."*

"Buenas noches," she says back, whatever that means.

I step a little closer and ask what her name is, *"Cómo se llama?"*

"Me llamo Lolita."

"Lolita," I repeat back to her, tryin' to say it just like she said it.

"Sí, Lolita."

Well, that's as far as my Spanish goes, so I hold out my fries to see if she'd like to try one. She takes one, tastes it, and looks as though she likes it. Then her brothers and sisters start lookin' at me, so I offer some to them, too. Their mama offers me a tamale, but it reminds me that I still have my burger and milk shake waitin' for me back at my table, so I take the tamale, and say the one last Spanish word I know, *"Adiós."*

"Adiós," they all yell back as I walk away.

When I return to our picnic table, I look at my family and say, *"Hola."*

Adriana looks at me. "Don't tell me you're going to start talking to us in Spanish now. It will be twice as annoying as that Southern accent of yours."

I suddenly remember one more phrase, *"No comprendo."* ("I don't understand.")

We awake once again to the sound of Daddy's megaphone blaring in our ears. "Up and at 'em, campers. Pack your bags and load them into the car—we will be departing directly from the boat launch after we spend one more glorious day in paradise." Daddy sounds really happy that this is our last day here.

I can smell the mornin' catch fryin' away on the stove again. Dino's had so much fun catchin' fish here, he says he's gonna come back when he's grown up and buy this place. It may be that long before he catches another fish. It doesn't come much easier than castin' on a small pond stocked with a million trout. Maybe Dino can make a living catchin' fish all day and sellin' 'em to the Something's Fishy restaurant. I have just never been able to eat anything that still looks like the animal itself. Take hamburgers. At least when you see those round blobs of beef cookin' away on the grill, they aren't in the shape of a cow. But fish, there's no gettin' around that. A fish still looks like a fish the whole time it's cookin'. Even if you cut the head and eyes off, you can still tell it's a fish.

I look for Lolita on my way out to the car, but I don't see anyone from her family. Maybe Sunday is their day off. That reminds me, we didn't go to Mass today, but I think God lets you off the hook when you're on vacation. We're all in kind of a mixed mood today. We're excited to go back to the dunes, but not so excited about seein' the relatives. Mama tells us to try and enjoy them anyway because once they head off to Italy, we may not get to see them for a long time. Daddy has a big grin on his face.

This time Uncle Nick is lettin' us go first to pick out the island. I think he's only doin' that so we'll be the ones to get stuck on the sandbar instead of him. It's fun to be the ones leadin' the expedition. It makes you feel like you're on *Mutual of Omaha's Wild Kingdom* and something wild could jump out at you any minute and drag you off. I hope they're attracted to the sparkly boat first.

After explorin' some new islands by boat, we find a really big one where the dunes surround a little cove, perfect for swimmin'. Everyone votes yes for that one, so we head for shore and beach the boats. While we're all helpin' to get the boats unloaded, I notice that Adriana has already disappeared. She told me this mornin' she was plannin' to ditch Stacy for the day so she wouldn't have to hear the next big fib *du jour*. But that leaves only me for Stacy to hang out with, which isn't exactly what I had in mind for my last day in paradise.

Just as me and Sailor head for the water, Stacy makes a beeline right toward me.

"Hey, A. J., want to go inner-tubing with me?"

I look around hopin' there's someone else named A. J. here, but I'm outta luck.

"Uh … sure." My brain isn't quick at comin' up with good excuses on a deserted island. It's not like I can say, "I gotta clean my room," or, "We're havin' comp'ny."

So we put our life jackets on and swim out a ways where the boat can circle around us. Sailor's howling from the shore because I abandoned him and told him to stay. Nicky tosses us the big inner tube that Stacy decided we're goin' double on, instead of goin' single on our own tubes like I wanted to do. Nicky must've told his dad that he wanted to drive 'cause Uncle Nick moves over and lets him have the driver's seat. Something about that bothers me.

We start out okay, each on our own half of the inner tube—even though my half is up in the air, and Stacy's is mostly underwater. So she yells, "Hit it," and Nicky guns the boat, and we go flyin' like we've been shot out of a cannon. Nothin' like whiplash right off the bat. I get the feelin' that this whole thing is a bad mistake. We go skiddin' across the wake so fast I see nothin' but spray in my face. It feels like someone is holdin' a firehose an inch in front of my nose and has it turned on full blast. Once we're completely outside the wake, Nicky thinks it's real funny to spin us at eighty miles an hour. The problem I have with that is, I'm on the outside, and when we get spun, I have my two-ton cousin slidin' right on top of me. So here I am trapped on this thing, gettin' the life squeezed out of me.

"Get off," I'm yellin' at the top of my lungs, but Stacy's just laughin' her fool head off like she's havin' the time of her life, and I'm about to lose mine.

Without even seein' it comin', we hit a boat wave and go sailin' through the air, but when we come back down, she pounds right back down on top of me. I start sayin' the Hail Mary and tell God to get ready for me 'cause here I come. He must've decided to give me mercy instead of my mansion, because right then we hit the wake again and flip completely over. Not wantin' to be dragged upside down, underwater, I release my hold from this rubber prison and am free at last.

Thank God for life jackets, because that is the only reason I am floatin' right now. I feel like a Raggedy Ann doll that just got tied and dragged behind a jet boat by someone's mean kid brother.

Daddy's been watchin' this whole thing from the island and is clearly upset by the time we were brought back to the cove. He wades out to meet the boat, and without so much as a word to big Nick or little Nick, he lifts my listless body out of the boat and carries me to shore. I must've swallowed half of the reservoir, 'cause I'm still coughin' and sputterin' while Daddy plops me onto a beach blanket to dry out. Sailor comes over and licks my face while I'm waitin' for my deflated body to reinflate. It takes awhile to recover from havin' the wind pounded out of you by someone three times your size. I'm relieved to see that Stacy is headin' straight for the food coolers, instead of in my direction.

Once I can finally breathe again, I make my escape over the sand dune with Sailor—before Stacy has a chance to finish eating. If she comes lookin' for me, there will be nothin' but a life jacket left behind, and I'll be long gone. When we reach the top of the dune, I realize we aren't alone on this island. On the other side is what appears to be an entire colony of people. I'm tryin' to figure out how they all got out here, 'cause I can only see one old boat pulled up onshore. It must've taken half a dozen trips back and forth to get everyone out here. I really need to get closer to the action to see what's goin' on down there.

Me and Sailor slide down the steepest part of the dune all the way to the shoreline. This is one of those dunes that plunges straight into the water, so we have to swim a ways to get to where the beach levels out. Once we've reached their shore, we climb out of the water and walk casually by their big gathering, as though we're just out for a beach stroll. There must be about twenty-five to thirty people here, all Mexicans, and havin' quite a time. Men are strummin' guitars, women are cookin' food over a fire, and right in the middle of everything is a tall pole with a *piñata* hanging down, surrounded by a zillion kids.

They all start singin' "Happy Birthday to You" in Spanish, and to my surprise, I hear, *"Feliz cumpleaños a Lolita."*

Sure enough, it's the same Lolita who makes our beds back at our motel. To think they are all here just to celebrate a kid's birthday makes me wish I was part of their big family. No one has ever made this big of a deal over my birthday. Out from the big circle of people, a little kid emerges with a blindfold on. Someone hands him a baseball bat, and he takes a big swing at the *piñata*. I want to play so bad I can hardly stand it.

Sailor suddenly spots a little scrap of a dog the size of a large rat and runs right through the middle of everything to chase it. The little yipper goes rippin' all over the place and finally hides under a beach chair. Then a bunch of kids run over to Sailor and start playin' with him. The grown-ups are lookin' around to figure out where the big dog came from, and here I am, lookin' guilty. They all seem pretty friendly about us crashin' their fiesta, and Sailor gets lots of pats and hugs from the little kids.

Lolita looks up and waves at me like she remembers me. She signals with her hand for me to come over. I'm not one to turn down a good party. Once I make my way over to her, everyone surrounds me wearing big smiles, and they just pull me right in like I'm one of their own. One really old woman keeps touchin' my hair, like she has never seen yellow hair before. It's not long before they have me eatin' fish tostadas and other strange things I would never eat at home, but they taste pretty good here.

The next thing I know, they've put a blindfold on me and are twirlin' me around 'til I'm so dizzy I feel like throwin' up my fish tostadas. Then they push me forward to try and whack the *piñata.* I start to swing the bat like a wild man, but I hit nothin' but air. Finally, I make contact with somethin', and everyone starts screamin'. I'm hopin' it's not a kid that I hit. When I take off my blindfold, I realize I've whacked open the *piñata,* and all the kids are divin' for candy. So I dive too. This is way more fun than Pin the Tail on the Donkey. Even Sailor's gettin' the hang of this and chomps down a piece of candy with the wrapper still on it.

I'm eatin' candy with Lolita when some little boy runs up and hits me, then runs away. I'm thinkin', *Hey, what's that for?* But Lolita pushes me to go after him. So I start to chase him, and other kids start runnin' around too. I finally swat him back, and everyone stops runnin' from me and starts runnin' from him. Now I get it—we're playin' tag. Before long, the whole place has gone mad. Kids are runnin' every which way, all over this island.

In the middle of all of this madness, I notice someone watchin' from the sidelines. I nearly break out in hives when I realize it's Stacy. I begin havin' inner tube flashbacks, and hearin' Nicky's sinister laugh. I don't care if they are my relatives, the Sophronias are evil. I don't know how long Stacy's been standin' there watchin' all of this, but it's not long before some kid runs up to her and tags her. I nearly have a cow when I see my cousin runnin' around, laughin', like I've never heard her laugh before—except when she was squishin' me to death on the inner tube. But this time, we're laughin' together.

After we're all worn out from playin' tag, Stacy starts givin' the little kids piggyback rides. This is a side of her I have never seen before. She shows them how to make a human pyramid and even volunteers to be on the bottom. I just don't get it how this snobby rich cousin of mine is havin' the time of her life without worryin' about lookin' cool to anyone. But the funny thing is, this is the first time she's ever looked cool to me.

We all sit around the big fire pit with all the moms and dads, aunts and uncles, grandmas and grandpas, brothers, sisters, cousins, and dogs like we are all just one big happy family. Stacy has all the little girls lined up, waitin' their turn to have their hair braided. She makes them all look so pretty, and their mamas just love it. I feel like I could just stay here all night and fall asleep to this guitar music, but my dream ends the minute I look up and see the *Big Fat Blue Baby* and *African Queen* comin' toward shore. It looks like a boat parade with all of *Fat Baby's* lights on. That's when I realize we must've been here a long time.

As they pull in near shore, almost everyone here

runs into the water to look at the bright blue jet boat. No one seems terribly impressed by our boat, except a few little girls. It is kind of a little princess boat. Daddy's callin' to me that it's time to go home. Me and Stacy look at each other, and I can tell she's as sad as I am about leavin' our new friends. All of the kids wade out to the boats with us to see us off.

I look at Lolita before climbin' into the boat. "*Adiós*" is all I can say.

"*Adiós mi amiga,*" she says back to me. Then we just look at each other like we know we'll probably never see each other again.

I see Stacy just standin' there watchin' us. Lolita looks at Stacy, and the next thing I know, Stacy throws her big arms around Lolita and hugs her, then turns, and wades out to her boat with tears in her eyes. I'm seein' things I never expected to see. All the kids are yellin' "*Adiós*" as she climbs aboard *Fat Baby Blue*. Daddy hoists me and Sailor into our boat, and we all wave good-bye as we begin our journey back home.

The one thing I can't seem to get out of my mind is how much happier Stacy was playin' with a bunch of kids who have hardly nothin', than she is when she's braggin' about how she has everything. She didn't even tell a single fib all day—not that she would know how to tell one in Spanish—but I don't think she even wanted to. I think she was just enjoyin' herself for once. It's funny how the people who I thought were very poor seem so much happier than the one who is very rich, but the one who is very rich seems happier playin' with the poor people, who really don't seem poor at all when you realize how much fun they have with each other. I'm not sure if I'm rich or poor, but I do know one thing, either way—*Life is good.*

12

Betrayal

It feels so good to sleep in my own bed again. The only thing that feels different is the weather. It seems to have dropped about thirty degrees overnight. It's so cold, not even Sailor wants to get up this morning. I have to push him off my blankets so I can climb out of bed. Hard to believe this is August. I half expect to look outside and see a freak snowstorm.

The weather isn't the only thing that seems weird. Danny didn't show up to go fishin' with J. R. this mornin'. He knew we were comin' home last night. I would think he would've been here first thing this mornin', but when I got up for breakfast, J. R. was still sittin' here waitin' for him. The fish will be all done with breakfast by now. That grabs my curiosity enough to take Sailor and head to the other side of the island to find out what's up.

When we reach Mr. Mueller's property, I stand outside the cabins watchin' for some kind of action, but no one is stirring. Even the little kids who are usually wild and noisy aren't makin' a peep. I'm thinkin' maybe they've all gone to shore, but the boat's still at the dock. Where *is* everybody? This feels too eerie, like something out of the *Twilight Zone:* **Family Disappears without a Trace**.

I can't just stand around all day waitin' for somethin' to happen, so I start back toward home.

When I reach the trailhead to the beach, I see someone standin' at the water's edge lookin' out at the lake. As soon as Sailor runs off wagging his tail, I realize it's Danny. I follow Sailor, hoping we aren't intruding.

"Danny?" I say, in a quiet voice.

He turns and looks at me. His face looks sad, like I've never seen it before, and his eyes have a world of hurt in them.

"Danny," I whisper, "what's wrong?"

Sailor licks Danny's hand, and he lays it gently on Sailor's head. "It's … my dad," he answers.

"Something's wrong with your dad?"

"Oh, something's wrong with him all right, but it's not what you would think." He takes a deep breath. "My mama got a call this mornin' from her friend who lives next door to us in Oklahoma. She told my mama that some other lady's car has been in our driveway every night since we left."

I have to think this through for a minute. "Are you sayin' that your daddy has been havin' a sleepover with another lady?"

"That's what I'm sayin'."

I can't imagine someone with a wife as pretty as Danny's mama havin' a girlfriend.

"Are you sure it isn't just a *friend* stayin' to keep your daddy comp'ny?"

"No, A. J., this woman's been trouble before, but my daddy *swore* …"

Danny turns his head away. He picks up a rock and throws it as hard as he can into the water.

I don't know what to say. I try and think of how I would feel if my daddy ever had a sleepover like that with someone besides my mama. But I just can't picture my daddy spendin' the night with anyone besides my mama—not in a million years.

Danny looks back at me. "I don't know how a man can do that to someone who loves him." He shakes his head. "I just don't know how my daddy could do that to my mama."

The rest of the day moves in slow motion. Me and Sailor walk Danny back to his cabin. I stand with him at the front door long enough to see all of his aunts in a huddle around his mama. The kids are all playin' board games on the floor, being told to "hush" when they get too loud.

The women are all yackin' back and forth on what they think their sister, Stella, should do.

"You need to go back and confront him."

"You stay right here. We can go pack your things and bring them back for you. You don't need to see that man again."

"Everyone leave her alone to decide for herself what's best." I side with Aunt Rebecca on that. I think it's best for me to say good-bye and go back to my cabin, but I want to know if Danny's gonna have to leave. It doesn't seem fair for him to have to go before his vacation is over. None of this seems fair to anyone. I don't even know this man, but I already don't like him. One person sure can mess things up for a lot of people.

"If you have to go home, Danny, come say good-bye to J. R."

"I will," he says, then closes the door.

When I get back to our cabin, Mama's sittin' at the table in her bathrobe, sippin' her mornin' coffee. I tell her what happened over at the Morgans'. Mama stops midsip and sets her mug down real slow on the table.

"A. J.," she says, "cover your ears, before you hear what I'm thinking about that man right now." She picks up her coffee again and takes another sip, probably to keep those thoughts from spillin' out in front of me.

"You shouldn't let that man make you think bad thoughts, Mama. You'll end up having to tell the priest all about it, word for word."

"Well then, I will tell him that the first word that came to mind can actually be found in the Old Testament."

"Then it can't be that bad of a word if it's in the Bible."

"No, kiddo, it's not, if it's used in its proper context; however, I might be using it out of context in referring to Danny's father."

"Well, what contest do they use it in, Mama?"

"That's *context,* A. J., and that context would be how the King James would refer to Balaam's donkey. I think we'd better leave it right there."

I don't think the priest could get too upset about

Mama referrin' to Danny's daddy as a donkey. I'll bet those priests have heard much worse in Grandma Juliana's confessions. I can't count how many times my mama has had to cover my ears when Grandma Juliana gets goin' on what Mama calls her "high horse." Grandma Juliana spends a lot of time on her high horse when it comes to talkin' about my daddy or Grandma Angelina.

I can tell Mama feels real bad for Danny's mama, but she says there's not much we can do to help in a situation of this kind.

"Well, Mama, I think maybe we could pray for her."

"Yes we can, A. J., *and* you'd better pray that Mr. Morgan never steps foot on this island within earshot of your mama."

It seems an eternity before Danny shows up on our front porch with the report of their plans. His mama and brother will go back to Oklahoma to deal with the whole big mess and pack her bags. Danny will stay on the island with his grandfather for now. He doesn't think he can face his daddy, so he'll wait here for his mama to return. Once she gets back to the island, they'll decide what to do from there.

This comes as a great relief to J. R. and me, as neither one of us wants Danny to leave. He isn't sure what Jason will do, but feels he will probably choose to stay in Oklahoma and help run the farm, since that's where his future is.

Of course, Adriana doesn't take the news very well. What hurts most is, Jason never comes to say good-bye to her before he leaves that afternoon.

I feel sorry for Adriana. I remember the words I heard Danny whisper at the potluck: "Like father, like son." They have some bad blood goin' on in that family, if you ask me. I just hope Danny escapes its curse.

The sun has now gone down, and I'm lyin' in bed thinkin' about what has happened to Danny's family. Somehow it reminds me of Grandma Angelina's cow.

When I was little, in the second grade, we went to visit Grandma Angelina and Grandpa Alfonso almost every weekend. Before Grandpa died, they lived on a farm, and they had this cow named Elsie. I watched Elsie grow from a baby into a mama. Every visit, I went out and petted Elsie and fed her dandelions from my hand. One day when Grandma Angelina and I were sittin' in the kitchen, a man in an old green pickup truck came up the drive. He stopped by Elsie's pasture and stepped out of his junky old truck with a rifle in his hand.

"What's that man doin' with a gun?" I asked my grandma.

"Oh, honey, he's here to put Elsie down."

"Put Elsie down? You mean shoot her?"

"Well, Angelina, that's what we raised Elsie for. That's how we get our food for the winter."

"What? You're going to eat Elsie?" I remember feelin' like I was going to be sick.

"It's really no different than the meat your mama buys at the store, honey."

"No different? This is your *pet,* for Pete's sake. You are going to eat your *pet.*"

I jumped up, darted to the window, and looked out. Just then a shot rang out, and I saw Elsie fall dead right before my eyes. *How on God's green earth could this happen?* Poor Elsie, betrayed by the very people she thought loved her.

That's how Danny's mama must feel right now. *"Pow!"* And Danny must feel like I felt, watchin' it happen before his own eyes, and not being able to do a thing to stop it.

I hate suffering of any kind. When I went to school the week after Elsie was assassinated, I told about it for Show and Tell. I told all about how the man came and shot poor Elsie. And how Elsie lay there with a pool of blood around her head, her eyes staring straight ahead like a zombie.

Mama came to pick me up at school that day because she had somethin' Grandma Angelina had asked her to deliver to the science teacher. When my teacher saw Mama in the hall, she asked if she could have a word with her. That always makes me nervous because it usually isn't to tell your folks what a great kid you are. Mama sent me out to wait in the car, where I got to try and guess what I'd done wrong *this* time. But when Mama got back to the car, she was grinning from ear to ear.

I was relieved that it didn't appear to be somethin' I'd be punished for. "So, what did she want this time, Mama?"

"Well, A. J., Miss Blazing was just sharing with me about your Show and Tell today. She thought it may have made some of those town kids a little queasy to hear all the details about poor Elsie—not having been raised in the country and all. Miss Blazing also mentioned how you sometimes remind her of little Wednesday Addams from *The Addams Family.*"

"Wednesday Addams? ... Like how?"

"Well, like the moth you found with a wounded wing, and insisted it must be 'taken out of its misery.' Then you stomped on it."

Mama was tryin' to look serious for my sake, but I could tell by the twinkle in her eye, she was doin' everything she could not to laugh at me.

"Well, first off, it wasn't a *wounded wing,*" I said, defending myself. "It had lost a *leg*, and I wasn't going to let it just limp around for the rest of its life on one leg, so I mercy killed it, that's all."

"That's okay, kiddo, I can live with a merciful moth killing now and then," she said.

"So, is that *all* you were smilin' about?" I asked.

"Well ..." a little rumble started up in Mama's throat ... "after your teacher finished telling me how you remind her of Wednesday Addams ..." the rumble turned to a high-pitched laugh that made it hard for Mama to get her words out.... "I pulled two frozen cow eyeballs out of my purse ... handed them to your teacher in a waxed paper baggie, and asked if she could give them to Mr. Biddle from Grandma Angelina. He had requested them for his science class.... If she thinks you're Wednesday Addams," Mama squealed, "then I must be Morticia."

Mama was laughin' so hard, she had to roll down the window and hang her head outside for more air. By now teachers and kids were pourin' out of the building to go home, and there was my mama in a full-blown laugh attack.

"Mama," I hissed, *"you gotta stop...."* But I knew it was hopeless. Then I saw Perry Perroni, the boy I've had a crush on all year, comin' right toward our car. Just my luck, we were parked right next to his mama's car.

"Mama, please stop," I begged, from under the dashboard where I was hiding. Then my worst nightmare came true. Perry stuck his head in my car window.

"Hi, A. J.," he said, then he took one look at Mama. I could tell he was thinkin', *Man, your mom is a loony.*

I will never understand this until my dyin' day, but at that moment I burst into a fit of laughter just like Mama. So, there we were, the both of us, hangin' out of our car windows like a couple of laughin' hyenas. That was the moment I first realized I had inherited Mama's laughin' genes and would be cursed for the rest of my life. It didn't much matter that the entire school body and faculty were watchin' us as they got in their cars to go home. If anything, it only made us laugh harder.

I'm lyin' here in bed rememberin' all of this with a smile on my face, but inside, my heart still aches for Danny's family.

I'm just about to fall asleep, when I hear music. It's awfully late for anyone to be playin' music right now. I climb out of bed and look down the hall, but there are no lights on anywhere. I'm sure I hear Tony Bennett. I know that voice anywhere. I make my way through the dark to the living room. Suddenly, I see two shadows moving across the floor in the moonlight. Mama and Daddy are in each other's arms, dancin' to "Fly Me to the Moon."

I shuffle slowly back to my room, then drift off to sleep listenin' to: "… Fill my heart with song, and let me sing for ever more. You are all I long for, all I worship and adore. In other words, *please be true*; in other words, I … love … you."

13

Downwind

The favorite part of my breakfast cereal is the colored marshmallow bits that float to the top when you pour the milk on. The problem with that is, you eat the best part right off the bat, and then you're stuck with a bowl full of boring cereal. Dino seems to think he's the cereal police in this family and rats on me if I try to sneak the boring part to Sailor.

One time I was even put on cereal restriction for pickin' all of the marshmallow bits out of the box before anyone else had a chance to have any. We were all at breakfast that morning, when I noticed everyone starin' down at their bowl of cereal like they were wonderin' where in the world all of the marshmallows were. I tried to look as puzzled as they did, as though maybe this box was a factory defect. Well, that only worked until Detective Dino ratted on me. I was stuck eatin' eggs and oatmeal for a whole week.

Breakfast cereal has been the cause of many of our family disputes. My mother refuses to buy the cereal with the free toys inside, even if it's the last box on the shelf. She wrote a letter to the cereal comp'ny one time, letting them know how she felt about their "sales tactics":

Dear Head Honcho of Marketing,

I would like to express my view as an All-American mother of five. I can appreciate the fact that your job is to sell cereal; however, I don't feel that it is in the best interest of the American family to use the sales tactics you have chosen.

Let's take a look at the big picture, shall we?

First, you have your "All-American Hero of the Month" plastered on the box cover munching away on Wheaty Flakes like there is no tomorrow. Great. All for it. But here's where you lose me: You add that "free toy inside" advertisement in the corner. Let's address that. Your "free toy" is not really "free," as it takes up nearly half of the box; hence, less cereal for the full price.

Now by advertising your "free toy," you have just created chaos in the grocery aisles, as kids are fighting and screaming over which box of cereal they want, not because of the cereal, but because of the dumb toy. I will give you credit for making it easier for me to find the cereal aisle when I go shopping, as I can walk in the front door of any grocery store, listen for all the screaming kids, and know exactly where to find the cereal in that particular store.

The fun doesn't really begin though until you

bring that box of cereal home and place it on your breakfast table in front of five adorable children. I would like to invite you to my home on a nice quiet Sunday morning before church so you can see for yourself how this works.

I know right now you may be thinking, "Lady, you don't have to buy the cereal with the free toy." Well, that's all fine and dandy, but I'm sure you know as well as I do that the cereal without the free toy is the stuff you sell to old folks who no longer care about toys, but rather their next bowel movement, and respectively, tastes like horse food.

I hope I have made my point: lose the toys, sell the cereal on the merit of its fine sugary taste that kids live for. One day when you stand before the Great Judge, you will not be held responsible for the Great Breakfast Battles of the American Family. At present, you are.

Warmest regards,
Sophia Juliana Degulio

My mama did get a letter back from the cereal comp'ny, but it was just a form letter thanking her for her interest in their products, along with coupons for more cereal. At that point Mama said, *"Que sera, sera,"* then recited the Serenity Prayer.

There were no breakfast battles today, because there is no one here but me and Sailor. I have just skimmed the marshmallow bits off the top of my cereal and am about to have the pleasure of passin' whatever I don't want off to Sailor.

The rest of the family has gone off to visit Grandma Juliana in town. Something "urgent" has come up again. Something "urgent" comes up about once a week with Grandma Juliana. It usually turns out to be something like, "The birdfeeder has run out of seeds, and the little darlings will starve."

My daddy has told her over and over, those birds are not *darlings*, they are *starlings*, but Grandma Juliana refuses to listen. Now we just call them Grandma Juliana's Darling Starlings. Daddy does not enjoy goin' to Grandma Juliana's house one bit, but he does it for Mama. Sometimes when we get stuck at Grandma Juliana's for too long, Daddy will do somethin' funny to make her stop whining, but it usually only makes her mad. The best time was when he stole her favorite spoon.

Grandma Juliana had this little silver spoon that she'd brought home from the Vatican in Italy. She kept it on display in her china cabinet in its "place of honor" and would brag about it every time we'd visit. One time when Grandma Juliana was goin' on and on about somethin', Daddy walked over to her china cabinet, opened the door, and slid the little spoon into his pants pocket like he was pretendin' to steal it. Well, that stopped her from whining all right, but she accused Daddy of bein' a "no-good thief" and has kept her china cabinet locked tight ever since.

No one knew what the "urgency" was about today, and no one gets terribly worried anymore when she calls with a new one. Lucky for me, I have a cold, and Mama says it's dangerous to be around old folks when you're sick because you might contaminate them.

The wind has just kicked up a notch, and I can't think of a better time to go driftin' than right now. Whenever Sailor sees me grab the life jackets, he takes off runnin' for the dock, then jumps in the boat and waits for me.

Mama told me not to go swimmin' with my cold, but she didn't say anything about driftin'.

I always bring the oars so we can row back when we've had enough driftin'. After laying the oars on the floorboard of the boat, we shove off.

Sailor likes to ride in back where it's not so bouncy if we hit boat waves. I like to lie on my back across the middle seat, close my eyes, and daydream. It's not always about Little Joe Cartwright. Today I'm dreamin' that me and Sailor are runnin' away to Europe. We are actually driftin' all the way there in this little dinghy of ours. Once we hit the European waterways, we get spotted by the European Coast Guard, and end up "LIVE" on the evening news all around the world: "American girl and her dog were rescued today by helicopter in the European Ocean." They show footage of me and Sailor being airlifted into the helicopter with one of those rope ladders. "What brave souls they are to have traveled all this way with only a gallon of water, ten peanut butter sandwiches, and a bag of Ahoy Matey chocolate chip cookies."

Once we're all warm and dry, we're given a Hero's Welcome by the Queen of France and are invited for a sleepover at the Royal Palace. The Queen loans me her favorite dress from when she was a small princess, and Sailor's given a royal bath and shampoo. He doesn't much care for the fancy ribbons they've tied to his ears.

We both get to dine with the Royal Family. Even Sailor gets to sit in a red velvet chair. They serve us french-dip sandwiches with french fries, and french pastries for dessert. The next morning the servants bring us french toast in bed on fancy little silver trays. Then we part with tears at the pier for our long journey back home. Everyone in Europe comes to send us off, throwing food and flowers into our dinghy.

Just as we are recrossing the European Ocean, a huge gust of wind snaps me out of my daydream and back to reality. To my surprise, I realize we've drifted all the way past the gas dock and are almost as far as the church.

"Sailor," I yell, "look where we are." Now I'm a little worried about how we're gonna row all this way back with the wind comin' against us.

I grab the oars, slide them into the oarlocks as fast as I can, and start to row. I'm rowin' with all of my might, and we are gettin' nowhere. Not only that, but the wind's gettin' stronger, and dark clouds are rollin' in above us.

It's just as far to the mainland as it is back to the dock, but I try and go toward home anyway.

My arms feel like they're gonna break off, and it's startin' to rain. I am so scared I can't think. "Oh, Jesus," I pray, "please send Your angels to help us. And make sure they know how to row."

I finally just give up with the oars and lay them back down so they won't get knocked into the water. I hunker down on the bottom of the boat and wrap my arms around Sailor. Then I bury my face in his fur and start to cry. We're just gonna have to drift until the storm blows over and hope that we're still alive.

Through the howl of the wind and the lapping waves, I never heard the sound of a boat motor, but when I look up I see it comin' toward us. A small boat with a motor on the back … Danny's fishin' boat—it's Danny and he's coming to save us.

I can't believe our luck. Actually, I don't believe in luck, but I don't believe Danny is an angel either. But he's here, and that's good enough for me. He pulls up alongside of our dinghy and grabs onto the stern. "Need a lift?" he calls out.

"Sure," I yell back.

"Take my hand and jump in."

I reach for his hand, and the instant he grabs mine back I feel safe, like I never want to let go of it. As soon as I land in Danny's boat, Sailor leaps in too. Danny takes the rope from our dinghy and ties it to the back of his boat. Then he takes off his jacket and puts it around me. We all head home with the cold wind and rain against our faces, but inside I feel warm.

By the time we arrive back at our dock, we are all drenched to the bone. Danny tells us to run for the cabin while he ties up our dinghy. He comes in after us, and I hand him a towel to dry off with.

"Do you have any wood to start a fire?" Danny asks.

I show him where the wood storage is next to the fireplace and hand him a box of matches.

"You'd better get some dry clothes on, A. J., before you catch pneumonia."

I go into the laundry room and toss all of my soppin' wet clothes into the dryer, then change into some clean dry ones.

By the time I return, Danny has the fire started. I'm thinkin' how cold he must be in all of his wet clothes, but I figure he's just gonna walk home in the rain anyway.

"Want some hot cocoa?" It's the least I can offer him for savin' my life.

"Sure," he answers, still fannin' the fire.

While I'm makin' the cocoa, I remember where Mama stashed the mini-marshmallows. That always makes cocoa so much better. I pile 'em about an inch high on top of the cocoa.

By now the fire is burnin' real good. We both sit right in front of the hearth on the sheep rug, drinkin' from our big warm mugs. I finally stop shiverin', but now my cough has started up real bad.

"I don't think that boat trip did your cold a lot of good," Danny says.

"Nope, probably not." I look at Danny pretty serious. "You aren't gonna tell my folks, are you?" *Mama might never let me drift again if she hears about this.*

Danny looks back at me and grins. "What's it worth to ya?"

"Your life."

"Well, in that case, I probably won't mention it."

"Thanks." *That's a relief.* "And thanks for savin' us." Then I ask, "How did you know we were out there anyway?"

"I was out fishin' when I saw you leave your dock, and I noticed you were nowhere in sight when the wind picked up. I figured you might need some help gettin' back."

"Good thinkin'. I didn't know if we'd ever make it back home."

Danny looks at me and starts to laugh.

"What's so funny?" I ask.

"You've got melted marshmallows all over your face."

"Well, it's hard not to when I have to stick half my face in the mug to get to the cocoa." Then, like a dummy, I ask when his mama's comin' back.

He tenses all up. "Not sure. My daddy's tryin' to talk her into stayin'. I knew he would. That's one reason I stayed here, to give her a reason to come back."

"Do you think she would really stay with him after what he did to her?"

"I don't know. She stayed last time, but this time she needs to leave or he'll never change. I'm not sure if she'll leave him though. He makes all these promises, and she starts to believe him, but he never keeps his word."

"I hope I never marry someone like that," I tell him. "I hope I find someone like my daddy. I don't think he would ever do that to my mama."

Danny got real quiet and just stared into the fire. "I think a good man would rather die than hurt someone that way."

I thought about that for a while. I hope I remember that when it's my turn to get married. Right now I just want to change the subject so he doesn't have to think about it anymore. "Hey, Danny, remember when you said you had a different dream than your brother for when you grow up?"

"Yeah."

"What is it?"

Danny looks at me. "I want to be a preacher," he says real quiet.

"Ah." *That's a nice dream.*

"How 'bout you?"

"I want to be a writer and a veterinarian."

"Really? Well, maybe we'll both get our dreams one day." Then he smiles at me, and for a split second, he reminds me of Little Joe Cartwright.

Once Danny figures that me and Sailor are gonna live, he heads back to his grandfather's cabin, but not before he piles the fireplace full of wood and makes me promise to stay off the water.

I curl up by the fire with Sailor sleepin' at my feet, wantin' to remember everything that just happened. When I return to school in the fall, this will be the story I will write about. This will be the one that my teacher will read to the class, instead of callin' my mama to discuss my summer vacation essay, like she did last year when I wrote about the trip my family had just taken to visit Grand Coulee Dam. My teacher wanted to know if Mama thought I was tryin' to be a smart aleck for writin' "Highlights from My Dam Vacation." Good grief. What was I supposed to call it?

Mama told her, "That's just the way A. J. would say it; and, yes, as a matter of fact, we really did have *dam burgers* at the *dam restaurant*, and we do have some *good dam pictures* to prove it if you would like to see them." Then she added, "Did A. J. happen to mention that she asked the police officer on duty if he was the *dam police?"*

This time I will call my story "The Day I Blew Away," and there will be no mistakin' my words by a teacher with cuss words on her mind.

14

Solitaire

Time passes way slower when I'm alone. I'm a little embarrassed to admit this, but sometimes when I'm by myself I still play with dolls. Troll dolls that is. I think they have the cutest little scrunched-up faces. I once saw a girl who looked just like one, but it wasn't as cute on her. My favorite troll doll's name is Abbey, short for Abigail—in honor of Sister Abigail. She has fluffy light pink hair and a tailor-made wardrobe by her own personal seamstress—me. I used to play with her all the time, but now that I'm older I have to be really bored first. More like desperate. But when there is absolutely no one else to talk to, my only options are a doll, a dog, or a hamster. At this point I think I'll round up all three. I have a feelin' it's gonna be a long night.

I know it's risky to sneak Ruby Jean into Papoose, but knowing Grandma Juliana, my family won't have a chance of gettin' home before midnight. This is how it works when you go to Grandma Juliana's house:

First, you have to battle all of the saint statues in her front yard. She has so many, it's like crossin' a minefield just to make it to the front door. It's especially tough if one of the statues is put there to ward one of you off, like St. Adelaide, patron saint for in-law problems, who was put there for my daddy. That's usually the one he trips over. Then there's St. Leonard of Noblac, patron saint against burglars. St. Gertrude of Nivelles, patron saint against rats. And St. Francis Borgia, patron saint against earthquakes. It's one thing to navigate these in the daylight, but you don't want to do this in the dark. I'm sure that's why the burglar statue has worked so well.

Once you're in, you get to deal with Grandma Juliana's latest crisis, which usually amounts to nothin'. Then she insists you stay for her ten-course Italian feast. Our last attempt to leave Grandma Juliana's without the feast was like bein' in one of those horror movies, where you try and escape but can't.

First, she pointed out the gigantic statue of St. Francis Caracciola, patron saint for Italian cooks, sitting on her kitchen counter. It was three times the size of her toaster. She told us this feast was sacred because St. Francis Caracciola had blessed it while Grandma Juliana was cooking. Then, she threatened that we'd all be damned to a long stay in purgatory if we didn't honor St. Francis and stay for supper. "It won't be long before I just drop dead," she yelled after us, on our way toward the door. Daddy told us to keep walkin', that as long as that statue of St. Aldegundis, patron saint against sudden death, is perched next to her bed, she doesn't have a chance of dropping dead anytime soon. I sure hope he's right since all of these statues have been willed to me.

Then, Grandma Juliana started in on Mama about how she was gonna have to buy herself a statue of St. Pelagius, patron saint for abandoned people, since her own daughter has chosen to abandon her mother. Mama started to get that crinkle in her forehead, which is always Daddy's cue that the guilt is settin' in ... again. Grandma Juliana is the only person on earth who can get to Mama that way. Mama will stay miserable for days once that happens, so Daddy figured he'd better give in.

"Dish it up, Mama J," he yelled back, then he turned us all around and whispered, "She should have been a travel agent; she's such an expert at guilt trips."

Grandma Juliana never heard him, she just thought we were all smilin' 'cause we got to stay longer. The only thing that made it tolerable to sit through an entire meal of nonstop whining was the spumoni ice cream that came at the end. Something about the green ice cream with the little nuts and red cherries helped to take my mind off of the sound of Grandma Juliana's droning voice. But I learned never to look at Daddy while tryin' to eat spumoni when Grandma Juliana is on her high horse. He made this face of pure agony, then crossed his eyes. I nearly choked to death on one of the nuts, tryin' not to laugh.

On the way out of the yard Daddy tripped over St. Adelaide again. Once we got into the car he told Mama that the day she starts to sound like her mother, he's shipping out to the Congo, where he will volunteer as a human target for the spear toss in the Wild Pygmy Olympics.

Grandma Juliana wasn't so bad when my Pappy Remo was alive. She was only up to two statues before he died. I think bein' alone can do funny things to people. Grandma Juliana was always a complainer, but at least when Pappy Remo was here, she had him to complain about instead of my daddy.

Pappy Remo liked to make his own peach grappa, which they tell me is like powerful fruit wine. He had his whole setup out in their garage, which drove Grandma Juliana crazy because she thought at any minute the police were going to pound on their door and haul them all away to jail, like in the prohibition.

Pappy Remo and Grandma Juliana were really first cousins, but Grandma Juliana will never admit it. He was a lot older than her too. On Pappy's eightieth birthday, we threw him a big party. He dragged his grappa-makin' setup right out on his open driveway and started makin' his grappa. Grandma Juliana had a fit and started ranting that the whole neighborhood could see it and this would be the day they would all be hauled away to prison. Pappy just looked at her and said, "Juliana, shutta you mout'. I'mma eighty years old; whatta they gonna give me … *life?*"

I miss my Pappy a lot. He didn't let many things ruffle him up, includin' his whining wife. He was the only one who could bring Grandma Juliana down from her high horse, but now that he's gone, she spends a lot of time up there. It's too bad when someone loses the only person that kept them from goin' completely nutty.

I hope I'm more like Grandma Angelina when I get old. She's just a happy old soul. She goes to this tiny country parish church where everybody brings in fresh flowers and zucchini to decorate the altar. When the Mass is over, you can take what you like home and cook it up for supper. Even with all those bright flowers layin' on that altar, you never feel like you're at Jesus' funeral like you do at Grandma Juliana's church.

The people at the country parish act like Jesus really did rise up from the dead and is gettin' things ready for us up there in heaven. We get to sing songs like, "Do Lord, oh do Lord, oh do You remember me, oh Lordy? Do Lord, oh do Lord, oh do You remember me?" Then you sing it again. Then it goes, "I got a home in Gloryland that outshines the sun, oh Lordy...." My other favorite song is, "When the Roll Is Called up Yonder." It just makes me want to be up there. I can hardly wait for the day when they get to the Ds in that Big Book of Life and I get to hear, "A. J. Degulio, come and get your mansion." I sure hope they know better than to use my real name. If I have to hear that name for all of eternity, I'll have to wonder if I'm really in heaven.

Ruby Jean always acts startled to be woke up in the middle of the day, but she's on her nocturnal schedule. Once I bring her into Papoose she perks right up. Sailor loves to watch her run around Troll Town. To him, Ruby is just a fuzzy roaming hot dog that he would love to chomp down if I weren't here watchin' him like a hawk. Instead he just licks her like they're best friends, but he can't help droolin' at the same time, which is a dead give-away that he'd rather just eat her. He's tryin' his best to be polite though. Ruby can only take so much of this dog bath business before she hides inside Lu Lu's Beauty Parlor to get away from him. Can't say I blame her. I'd want a shampoo and 'do too if I'd just been slobbered on by a giant dog tongue. A wet hamster is not a pretty sight. All of her skin shows through and she looks like a newborn rat.

I give Ruby a little wash and fluff before she heads off to the snack bar for some peanut butter. Probably a good thing she stays away from the Cut-n-Curl Salon.

About the time the sun goes down I figure it's time to put Ruby Jean back in the shed. I give her furry little head a kiss and tuck her back in for the night, although nighttime is really when a hamster's day begins. At least she's off to a clean start.

The fire is just a heap of glowing coals now. It makes me so drowsy I feel myself startin' to drift off. I try and say a few prayers while I'm still a little bit awake. The last thing I remember is thankin' God that I'm here instead of at the bottom of the lake. I don't know how long I've slept when I hear the sound of our boat motor, then familiar voices comin' through the door. I recognize a few blurred faces. "How's Grandma Juliana?" I mumble, still half asleep.

Adriana is the first to respond. "You *don't* want to know."

J. R. says, "Consider yourself lucky you were sick."

Dino says, "Ditto."

Benji says, "Double ditto."

Daddy looks at me and crosses his eyes like when we were eatin' spumoni and says, "Wonderful as usual, A. J., just *wonderful.*" He smiles at Mama, who looks like she just needs to take an aspirin and go to bed.

"How're you feeling, kiddo?" Mama asks, soundin' real tired. She leans down and touches my forehead like moms always do when you're supposedly sick.

"I'm good," I answer back, *tryin' not to sound like I took the boat out on the water during a windstorm and nearly got swept away for good.* "Nothin' much happened around here today," I add, *other than I had to be rescued and towed home by the neighbor boy who saved my life.* "Just laid around all day with Sailor," *and my troll doll that I'm too embarrassed to admit I still play with, and my hamster who's hidin' out in the shed.*

"Sweet dreams," says Mama, and kisses my guilty little forehead.

"Sweet dreams too, Mama."

I'm so comfortable right where I am, I just fall back to sleep dreamin' of boats, and wind, and Ruby, and Grandma Juliana, and wild pygmies.

15

Dear Friends and Deer Heads

My best friend moved next door to me on the snowiest day last winter. We didn't start out as best friends, even though we had a lot in common. Dorie was the Recess Queen of her class, and I was the Recess Queen of mine, so we were kind of in competition from the get-go. But that wasn't all. We also liked the same boy. Perry Perroni. He was, by far, the cutest boy ever to walk the halls of Squawkomish Elementary School. The difference between me and Dorie is, I'm shy when it comes to boys. She isn't. So up until the day Dorie came to Squawkomish Elementary, there was just a silent understandin' that Perry and me were paired up. He always picked me to be on his team or to have tea parties with him at four square. He would keep hittin' the ball back to me real nice until kids started teasin' him. Then he'd turn all red and hit it to someone else.

But then one day Dorie showed up and not only decided she liked Perry, but told him and everyone in the whole school that she liked him. The thing about forward girls, they might get who they want for a while, but they just move on down the line after they ruin a perfectly good romance like the one me and Perry had. Perry fell for her, all right, and was havin' tea parties with her instead of me. I had to pretend this didn't bug me, but it did, so I took up tetherball instead. Well, it was only a week before Dorie dumped Perry for someone else. By the time Dorie moved next door to me, she'd had tea parties with just about every guy in the fourth grade.

So when that movin' van pulled up next door to our house in December, I was not at all happy to see that it was Dorie movin' in. But the strangest thing happened. Over Christmas break, she rang my doorbell and asked if I wanted to go sleddin' with her. If I hadn't been so bored out of my mind I would've said no, but I was, so I went. We stayed out way past dark and had the greatest time flyin' down hills together, tippin' over, laughin', and startin' all over again. When we finally got called in for the night, Dorie invited me to sleep over. We stayed up until three in the morning talkin' about everything two nine-year-old girls could possibly talk about. It started out with boys, and ended up with boys, but in between, she told me somethin' that really made me think different about her. She told me she didn't have a dad. She *did* have a dad, but he was killed in the Vietnam War in 1966. After her dad died, she and her mom ran out of money, so they had to move in with her grandma until they saved enough to buy the house next to ours.

I'll never forget Dorie's sad eyes when she told me that story. From then on somethin' inside me started to like her, even if she did steal my boyfriend. It made me think that maybe she was just so lonely, and all those boys just reminded her of her dad in a way. We've been best friends ever since that night.

As for Perry Perroni, he's tried to win me back ever since he got dumped, but I won't give him the time of day. When he tries to hit the ball to me in four square, I just hit it to someone else. Usually another boy. Even though I still have a secret crush on Perry, I will not let anyone mess with my heart like that. I believe in loyalty—especially after everything I've seen on this island lately.

Being away on this island makes me miss my friends back home, especially Dorie. But one thing we promised each other was that we'd write letters back and forth. Since my cold has gotten worse—*for some mysterious reason that may involve boats and rain and wind*—my mama has been watchin' me like a hawk and keepin' me off of the water. Seems like a good time to keep my promise to my best friend.

Hi Dorie, Dorie, Bo-Borie, Banana-Fana, Fo-Forie,

How is your summer going without me? Anything new in the neighborhood? Is Miss

Peepers still spying on everyone? We've been calling her that for so long I can't remember what her real name is. Miss Peepers fits her so perfectly. Too bad she never got married and had ten kids so she'd have something better to do than spy on us all the time.

What is she so worried about anyway? Does she think we're trying to poison her little bunny rabbits or something? All we ever do is feed them carrots and old lettuce. She should know if they aren't dead by now, that we obviously aren't trying to poison them.

So, here I am stranded on Gilligan's Island with Miss Glamour Queen Ginger for a sister. My only salvation is having Sailor and Ruby Jean here. I'm so worried my parents might find out about Ruby. Adriana's threatened to squeal on me if I ever squeal on her for kissing Jason the two-timer. Jason is nothing like his little brother, Danny. Danny is like the perfect big brother I never had. Don't tell blabbermouth Cindy, but Danny looks like a blond Little Joe Cartwright, AND he saved my life when Sailor and me got swept downlake. Don't worry, he's way too old for me. Maybe when he's 100 and I'm 97 we could go steady. Then it won't seem like we're that far apart in age.

So, did your Hammy have her babies yet? Can't wait to see them. I hope they're really ugly so I won't want one. You know I'm a sucker for anything cute and fuzzy. I get so worried about keeping Ruby Jean out there in the shed. Sometimes I think I should just mail her to you in a box with air holes and let her stay at your house. I could come over every day after school to see her. You are so lucky to have a mom who likes rodents. Wish mine did.

Well, before I go 100% crazy here with no friends to talk to ... WRITE BACK ... or else. Or else, I will tell every living person on earth that you have a crush on Steven Crammer bigger than the sky — except when he wears those dorky striped pants. His mom probably makes him.

Toot-a-loo,
A. J. for "Ain't Jokin'"

P.S. I sure miss watching the pizza truck pull up to nosey Miss Peeper's house whenever J. R. phones in an order for her. You would think they would have caught on by now. Maybe she actually pays for them and eats them. I wonder if she liked the one with anchovies. I'm getting hungry just talkin' about pizza. Too bad they don't deliver on Islands. You could send one to me, and I'd say, "Hey, I never ordered this." And they'd say, "Well, as long as we had to come all this way, you can just have it." As Miss Peepers would say, "You pranksters." She is just like Gladys Crabbits on "Bewitched." We could call her "Gladys Crabbits and her rabbits."

P.S.S. The bad news here is that Danny's dad had a sleepover with some lady when Danny's mom was here on the island. Isn't that rotten? I *don't know his name, but my mom just calls him BD. Short for Balaam's donkey.*

The deal with Miss Peepers is that she's just a really snoopy lady. And, she happens to live right across the street from us, which makes us an easy target. Since we know she is always watchin' us from behind her pink curtains, we make sure we wave to her every time we leave the house.

Since the time we were little, she has blamed every single thing that happens in her yard on us. Whenever one of her flowers was missing, which she must have counted to know one was missing, she would call my mom and tell her that her little hoodlums have been pickin' her flowers. Or if any cat did its business in her sand garden, she blamed it on our old cat that couldn't walk that far if he wanted to, and she expected us to come clean it up. The last time she ever called was right after old Charlie died, and Daddy let her know that unless cats really do have nine lives, there was a pretty good chance it wasn't ours.

Those are the kind of things that tempt you to play pranks on people like her. Our pranks are pretty harmless. Besides J. R.'s pizza deliveries, the twins like to sneak over and pour the water out of the vase on her front porch that holds her cattail swamp foliage. After a few days without water those things explode. All of their fluffy white stuffin' comes poofin' out of them. It's pretty cool, really.

The best thing that ever happened to Miss Peepers was right after we brought Sailor home from the pound. We couldn't have planned this better ourselves. Sailor likes to play out in the woods behind our house. One time he came home with something that looked like a deer skull with a little bit of fur still attached. Miss Peepers had left her front door open while she was out waterin' her lilies. Sailor walked straight into her front room and left the deer skull right there on her white carpet, like he was bringin' her a special gift. We didn't know about any of this until someone rang the doorbell and Mama went to answer it. Miss Peepers was standin' there on our front porch, holdin' this grungy deer skull with her garden gloves. She looked at Mama and said, "Your dog just deposited this on my white carpet. I believe it belongs to you." Then she just dropped it right at Mama's feet, turned, and walked away. Mama said that was the *darndest* thing that's happened in a long time. Daddy called it serendipity.

The neat thing about sendin' a letter to Dorie is that my dad takes it with him when he goes to work in the morning and swings by our neighborhood to check on our house in town. If Dorie is home, he gives her my letter in person; then if she writes back real fast and gives it back to him before he leaves, I get her letter when Daddy gets home from work.

Dear A. J.,

Mrs. Sharp took the plate of cookies and said, "If you girls would like a quick swim, I can only watch you for a half hour."

We tried to act all surprised

like that was the last thing on our minds. Of course we were in that water in no time flat. We had underwater tea parties and did cannon balls and swan dives off of the diving board. I only flubbed up with one belly flop. OUUCH.

Guess who we saw at the WIGWAM STORE last week? Stuck-up Marcie Walker. Me and Cindy just smiled at her like now we know where she buys all of her cheap clothes. She tried to pretend she was only there because her mom was shopping. Well, Cindy found the same shirt that Marcie was wearing on one of the racks and yelled across the store, "Hey, Marcie, look. It's the same shirt you're wearing."

It's no big deal if we shop there because we don't pretend to be all rich and snobby like she does. She even makes fun of poor kids who have to shop there. She won't be able to make fun of anyone in front of us anymore, or she'll be sorry.

Well, I'm writing you back, but I already told the whole world, including Steven Crammer, that I like him, so it wouldn't matter if you told anyone, anyway. You'd better write back or I WILL tell all of Squawkomish that you're in love with an older man.

Your Best Friend 4 ever,

Dorie

16

Big Island Bash

It's officially tradition. Anything that happens more than once in this family is considered tradition. Big Island Bash started last summer on August 10, in honor of my mother refusin' to live the life of a hermit. About the time Sophia Loren hit the heights of stardom, my mama hit an all-time low. She told my daddy that there was something wrong with having her *impostor* get away with living the high life, while she was stuck on this island with five runny-nosed kids and no friends all summer.

That's when my daddy said, "Soph, the world is your stage. Write yourself a script, and let me know when opening night is."

That's when Mama came up with Big Island Bash. It's become her "baby," and everyone just goes with the show or moves outta the way.

She plans the food, the music, the theme, then invites half the world. She says only half of the world's people know how to have fun; the other half are just put on earth for contrast.

Her traditional party theme is A Tropical Island Paradise, and she insists everyone "dress accordingly." Then she hires this wild-lookin' jungle band to play steel drums and boogie music. The invitations go out two weeks ahead, so everyone has time to hunt up some grass skirts, muumuus, and plastic flower leis.

The invites were the cause of Grandma Juliana's recent *urgency*. She called Grandma Angelina to brag about her upcoming trip to Italy, knowing how jealous that should make her. But Grandma Angelina told Grandma Juliana that she could tell her all about it at the "kids' party," just to get her off of the phone. That's when Grandma Juliana asked, "What party?"

After last year's disaster, my daddy banned Grandma Juliana from the guest list. She followed him around the entire party, blaming him for turnin' her youngest daughter into a "Bohemian Jungle Woman." She just couldn't grasp the concept of *pretend* and whined about her "Little Sophia" becoming a disgrace to her Italian heritage by running around with a bunch of wild jungle animals for friends.

Grandma Angelina, on the other hand, had a great time winning the limbo, which was pretty amazing for someone sixty years old.

Once the cat was out of the bag and Grandma Juliana realized she wasn't included this year, she declared a national family crisis. That was the day I drifted downlake. Of course my quick-thinkin' mama told Grandma Juliana that she just knew how busy she must be plannin' her trip to the Old Country and didn't want her to feel obligated to come.

Grandma Juliana thought it only fair that she be given the right to turn down the "Bohemian Monkey Party" on her own initiative. It only added to the grudge she already had for Grandma Angelina, but that is an ongoin' lost cause anyway. As Mama always says about things like this, *"Que sera, sera."*

The best part of the whole bash is that everyone's kids are invited too. By the time all the families show up, there are so many kids runnin' around this island, it looks like the Planet of the Apes. The only thing I don't like is havin' to wear this dumb grass skirt over my bathin' suit. Mama dressed me like one of those little hula dancers on the dashboard of cars, then propped me up next to a flaming torch to welcome the guests.

I'm the official greeter. J. R. is in charge of tying up the boats and lightin' the tiki torches. The twins are ice runners for when the ice runs out. They have to keep refillin' the ice buckets all night long. Adriana offers each of the women a fresh flower for their hair. Of course she has worked on her own hair for hours and spent most of the day in front of the mirror decidin' which side to wear her flower on. She couldn't decide if she wanted to be *available* or not. One side means you are; the other side means you're not. She will probably switch it back and forth all night—available for the cute guys, unavailable for the dorks.

Oh my gosh. Speakin' of dorks … here come the Gizmodes. I want to run and hide. They are one of those families that look like their name. There are three boys, who all think they are Greek love gods, as Adriana puts it. The two oldest try and outdo each other to impress her, and it just makes Adriana gag. The youngest one always comes after me.

Last year, he chased me all around the island after his brother told him he'd give him a dollar if he kissed me. He never got it though 'cause I kicked him so hard in the shins he finally gave up. If he tries anything this year, I'm gonna sic Sailor on him.

I've been practicing with Sailor all week, just in case. I took this old stuffed bunny and set it across the yard. Then I'd yell, *"Sic'm Sailor,"* and Sailor would charge across the yard and rip that rabbit to shreds. I'm almost hopin' I'll get to test him out on the Gizmode kid.

The oldest boy is swankin' his way over to Adriana right now. "Well, hello there," he says, tryin' to sound like Don Juan. "How about a traditional Hawaiian kiss?"

I want to say, "This isn't Hawaii, you idiot," but Adriana saves me.

"A. J., why don't you show the Gizmodes to the obstacle course you and the boys were working on earlier?"

Oh man, not me.

Then Adriana winks at me, and I remember. "Oh, yeah, the *obstacle course*. Right this way, guys." I make sure Sailor is right on my heels the whole time. The boys and me have been workin' on games all day for all the kids, but we rigged the obstacle course especially for the ones who need some coolin' off.

I signal to J. R. to come over and help explain the course to the Gizmodes. Meanwhile the steel drums have started up, and people are beginnin' to boogie. This is good. No one will be able to hear those Gizmodes screamin' their heads off once we're finished with them.

J. R. starts to walk them through the course, explainin' that we'll be keeping time to see who completes the course the fastest. "A. J. will be at the finish line to clock your time," he says.

The Gizmodes insist they want to run it all together and that anything goes to stay in the race. J. R. and I smile at each other. This is even better than we expected; this way no one will have to miss out on the grand finale.

I take my place at the finish, slowly lookin' up at the fifty-five gallon drum of ice water that J. R. has carefully rigged overhead. A six-foot steel rod runs right through the drum and is secured into the tree. A long rope pulley is attached to the lip of the drum and dangles within an arm's reach of me.

The riggings all look to be in place and secure. I give J. R. a thumbs-up. Prepare for Operation Ice Bath.

J. R. gives the signal: "Ready, set, go."

The Gizmode brothers are on their way. They have tires to climb through, balance beams to cross, high jumps and low jumps to make … and these guys are brutal with each other. They shove and push one another out of the way as hard as they can. A small crowd of kids has gathered to cheer them on. No one's real sure which one to root for, since they are all equally weird. There's just a lot of "go, go, go" goin' on.

After a rough romp through the forest, they are finally stumblin' their way to the finish line. Luckily, all three are neck and neck with one another. Even Adriana and the twins have come to cheer them on to victory. It's nice to know there are still certain things that unite our family. Putting the Gizmodes on ice is one of them.

The instant they cross that finish line, J. R. pulls that rope with one quick jerk, and *voilà*, Operation Ice Bath is a success. We are all hootin' and doublin' over with laughter. Adriana leans toward me and whispers, "That oughta cool their jets for a while." The funniest part is that the Gizmodes are laughin' as hard as the rest of us. They really are a buncha kooks. At least we can't get in trouble if they think it's funny too. I don't even think it counts as a sin when that happens.

I make my way around to all the newcomers I'd missed while I was away at the races. Most of them are hangin' out by the boogie band, just standin' around. Then Mama steps in and gets them all goin'. Mama doesn't believe that life should be a spectator sport and, boy, is she shinin' tonight. She is in her *element*, as she calls it. She gets out there just a boogyin' and twirlin' her heart out. She's wearin' a bright orange flower in her hair and swingin' a big tumbler of tropical punch in her hand. A tiny paper umbrella is stickin' out of a chunk of pineapple with a cherry to boot, all lookin' like Hawaii in a glass.

It makes me happy to see Mama so happy. Daddy just stands back watchin' it all with a smile.

As soon as it starts to get dark out, a group of us kids gather under a tiki torch for a round of Truth or Dare.

When it comes to my turn, I pick *truth*. You never want to get stuck with a *dare* at a party like this. The peer pressure is awful, and either way you end up lookin' like a fool. So little Rodney Gizmode asks me, "What's your greatest fear?"

Well, duh, that's easy. "Gettin' stuck in the confessional at church."

After a bunch more dumb *truth* questions, we finally get someone to take a *dare*. The little kids don't know better. It's J. R.'s turn to give the *dare*.

"Hold on," he yells, and runs back to the cabin, returning with the megaphone my daddy uses to evacuate parks when there are park fires.

J. R. takes everyone through the woods to the outhouse that all the party guests use. We all stake out about thirty feet behind it in some bushes. Then he takes the little kid right up behind the outhouse and hands him the megaphone. "What's your name, kid?" J. R. asks.

"Timmy," he answers boldly, for someone who doesn't know better.

"Okay, Timmy …" J. R. begins to instruct him, but we can't hear what he's sayin' from where we are. Then J. R. comes runnin' back to our group and tells us all to "*hush up.*"

A few minutes go by, then we see Flo, Mama's hairdresser, go into the outhouse. Timmy is crouched down low behind the outhouse, directly behind the seat. J. R. waits until he thinks the timing is right, then gives Timmy the signal.

Timmy sticks the megaphone along the bottom of the outhouse and yells, "H-e-e-l-l-p, I've fallen in. Get me out; it stinks down here."

Five seconds later, Flo comes flyin' out of there, screamin' at the top of her lungs, "Someone's fallen in … someone's fallen in—get Sonny."

As soon as we hear the name *Sonny*, we run for our lives down to the beach. We sit around the bonfire actin' like we never heard a thing. J. R. has to stash the megaphone 'til the coast is clear for him to return it to the cabin. After things seem to calm down we make our way back to the party to check out the food. Mama has her traditional party pig twirlin' over the BBQ pit with an apple stuck in its mouth. I have never seen anything so disgustin' in my life. Grown-ups come up with some of the weirdest ideas if you let them do whatever they want. I start at the dessert table first and make my way through the line backward. If I'm gonna fill up on something, I'd rather fill up on desserts and be too full for the salads—and I'm goin' nowhere near that pig.

Everyone seems to be enjoyin' themselves. Daddy's startin' to set up the limbo bar for after dinner. Adriana is surrounded by boys, all tryin' to dance with her, sit by her, or eat with her. She doesn't seem very interested in any of them. That's a first for Adriana.

I'm lookin' around, takin' it all in, when suddenly I see Danny. He's not alone either. Right next to him, dressed in a floral muumuu, is his mother. Danny's mama is back from Oklahoma.

I run over and tell Mama that Danny's mama has come. She puts down her dinner plate and goes to welcome her to the party. Adriana sees them and comes hurrying over. She asks if Jason came back too, but Danny says Jason stayed to help his dad with the farm. Adriana looks away, sad, then walks off by herself toward the beach. I think Jason means more to her than any of her other island guys.

My mama takes Danny's mama under her wing and leads her over to the food and drink table. Mama's always been good with hurtin' people. She treats them like I treat wounded birds. You have to be very delicate with them.

"Your mama came back," I say to Danny.

"She left him," Danny corrects me.

We look at each other, and I can see the relief in his eyes. "Hungry?" I ask him.

"Yeah," he says, matter-of-fact.

I take him over to join the feast. J. R. sees Danny and comes over and sits with us. He fills Danny in on all the good stuff he'd missed before he got there, like the Gizmodes and Truth or Dare. The way he told it, he had Danny laughin'. It was nice to hear Danny laugh again.

Everyone was real glad to have Danny's mama back. But Adriana never returned to the party once she found out that Jason didn't come back. Here were all of these guys swarmin' around Adriana all night, and the only one she wants is the one she can't have.

Danny and J. R. go runnin' off somewhere, so I just wander around with Sailor, watchin' everything that's goin' on. There must be about a hundred people at this bash, and they're scattered all over the island. Most of the grown-ups are over by the jungle band and food tables. Kids are either playin' the games we'd set up or down at the bonfire roastin' marshmallows. But the one thing that brings everybody to the same place at the same time is the limbo.

One problem. Daddy goes to look for his megaphone so he can round up all the guests. It's still stashed in the bushes. I go runnin' to tell J. R. and finally find him in a rock-skippin' contest with Danny.

"J. R., you'd better hightail that megaphone back to the cabin or Daddy's gonna have your hide." Daddy has already warned us that messin' with government equipment is a federal crime and to be considered PBD: punishable by death. I hope he was kiddin'.

J. R. is runnin' as fast as he can when he almost runs right into Daddy on the way to the cabin. I come runnin' up behind him to try and save his life. "Hey, Daddy, J. R. thought you might want to use the megaphone to round up the gang for the limbo."

Daddy looks at J. R., then at the megaphone, then at me. "Uh-huh," he says, and reaches for the megaphone. He walks away, starin' back at us with *that look*, and says, "PBD, J. R."

This may be the last night I'll be seeing my brother on this earth.

When we show up at the limbo, the music is in full swing, and the limbo line wraps around the band in a huge circle. For some reason, Flo isn't joining in. She's probably sittin' over there wonderin' if she's lost her mind, hearin' voices that aren't there. Poor Flo. Must've been pretty nerve-rackin' to bring Daddy all the way to the outhouse and not hear anyone yellin' anymore. Maybe she thought he drowned by the time Daddy got there.

The real problem here is that Daddy shouldn't have any trouble figurin' this one out. He's the one who told us about this trick. He did the same thing to someone once himself.

The limbo is my favorite event of the whole bash, next to watchin' the Gizmodes get soaked. I'm just standin' under the tiki torch, feelin' the rhythm of the drums comin' up through my feet and all the way out my ears. I can feel the ground move beneath my toes, and they start tappin' on their own. My body starts to move to the beat like there's no way it's gonna hold still as long as those drums are playin'. I start boogyin' through the line with everyone else, and they can't hold still either. We are all movin' like one long centipede around the band and under that limbo stick. Even if I wanted to stop, I'll bet my feet would just walk off without me, and my body would shimmy away to follow. But I don't want to stop. I think God put this rhythm inside of people so when we hear that music, we know just what to do without even takin' lessons. I'll bet He's smilin' down on us right now. I think He likes to watch His kids dancin' around and havin' fun. It's nights like this I'm glad I have a mama who won't settle for boring. And a God who makes the beat of the drums for us to dance to.

17

Mouth of Babes

Catechism is taking a good long time to get over with. I'm sittin' at this little desk writin' all my sins on the desktop with the back of my eraser. This way, I'll remember them all when I go to confession. That strikes me kind of funny because in a few minutes, when I go into confession, God really will erase them all for me. I'm picturing Him up there with this giant eraser and can't help gigglin' to myself.

"Angelina?" Sister Abigail says real sweet. *Does she always have to call me that?*

"Yes, Sister?" I answer.

"Is there something funny you'd like to share with the rest of the class?"

"Ummm, not real …" Everyone's lookin' at me like they are dying of boredism; it makes me feel sorry enough for them that I decide to go ahead and share. "Well, *yes,* Sister, I was just writin' all my sins down here on this desk with my eraser, and all of a sudden I thought of God with this giant eraser, and ..."

People are startin' to give me funny looks, like they're makin' fun of my vision.

"Never mind," I say. "Y'all can just go back to bein' bored."

"Class," says Sister Abigail, "Angelina has a point here that I think we should all take to heart. Why do you think we go to confession anyway?"

Jorgan Junker raises his hand.

This should be good, since he's got the longest list of sins ever known to man.

"My grandpa says, if we die before we confess all of our sins, we'll get a one-way ticket straight to hell. But if we go to confession, we can trade in our ticket for a ticket to heaven."

"Your grandpa's an idiot," Sam Starks yells.

"Is *not.*"

"Is *so.*"

"*Yeah?* Well, I'm not takin' *any* chances," Jordan yells back. "Can I go to confession now, Sister?"

No way, buddy. You're not goin' before me again. While Sister Abigail is busy tryin' to settle everyone down, I bolt for the door. I'm not waitin' in there again for Jorgan Junker to trade in his ticket.

For once I'm first in line. Lookin' around I see J. R.'s class linin' up behind ours. Sure enough, right behind J. R. is little Rodney Gizmode. It gives me the creeps just seein' him again. My daddy has to work with his daddy, which is why we have to invite their family to our bashes. I'm just about to go into the confessional when I see Rodney whisperin' something to J. R., and they both look over at me smilin'. Something is up, but I've gotta go in there and close that door behind me.

Father Patrick is all ready to hear my confession first, which is a relief, 'cause the second I get out, I'm findin' out what those two are up to. I finish up, feelin' pretty good about my shorter-than-usual list of sins, and head for the door. I push on the little handle, but nothin' happens. I push harder still, but it's jammed shut. Then it hits me. J. R. and the Gizmode kid were both playin' Truth or Dare at the bash when I told everyone my greatest fear.

That does it, right there. I start poundin' on that door like there's no tomorrow. There is *no way* I'm gettin' trapped in this dark hole again. "Get me out, GET ME OUT OF HERE!" I scream. Suddenly the door flies open, and here I am facin' an entire line of people, all starin' at me like *I'm* the crazy one here. Then I see Sister Abigail holdin' the doorstop that *someone* must've slid under the door when I was inside.

"I'll kill you, Rodney Gizmode," I yell and charge after him. He flies out of the sanctuary and down the hall. I chase him until his daddy's car pulls up, and he jumps in. I leave church with only one thing on my mind: *Revenge. There is always next year's Big Island Bash, Rodney Gizmode.*

Mama and Mrs. Morgan have become soul sisters. *Sophia and Stella.* They sit out on our dock together every afternoon with their iced tea and potato chips, chitchattin' and laughin' themselves silly. Mama says laughter is the best medicine and will not put up with someone bein' a sour-puss. "Life is much too precious to waste it looking like you're sucking on a dill pickle," she says, whenever one of us is bein' grumpy. She's makin' sure that Mrs. Morgan has plenty to laugh about.

Mama took Mrs. Morgan shoppin' in town yesterday and made her play the Sophia Loren game. Mrs. Morgan said she's had more fun since she came to this island than she's had in years. She must not get off that farm much back in Oklahoma.

They are both gabbin' away on the dock, and I'm sittin' here pretendin' not be listenin', but of course I am. A good journalist knows how to get the scoop without anyone suspectin' it. I'm playin' with a stick in the water just to look busy.

Mama asks Mrs. Morgan what Mr. Morgan's first name is. When she says, "Jack," Mama just about has a cow right here on this dock. "*Jack?* Jack. How apropos. I was just tellin' A. J. that he reminds me of Balaam's donkey in the King James."

They're both laughin' so hard, they're spillin' their iced tea all over the place. I'm still tryin' to get the joke. Grown-ups laugh at the weirdest things.

I think Mama is givin' Mrs. Morgan lessons on how to be a strong, happy woman. Then she won't go runnin' back to Jack the minute he calls her up on the phone. That's what everyone is worried about, especially Danny. Mrs. Morgan told Mama it will take more than a phone call to get her to go back.

"You're darn tootin' it will," Mama says. "He'll have to drag you back to Oklahoma over my dead body. Stella, there are some things a woman should never have to tolerate, and that little slumber party that went on in your home was a splendid example. A man like that should be given two options in life after a stunt like that: to be tarred and feathered, or fed to the lions for sport. Take your pick, buddy...."

Mama keeps on talkin', when suddenly I notice a shadow across the dock. I turn around, and there is this man standin' right behind us just listenin' to everything Mama's sayin'. He's a big man, real rugged like.

"Mama," I rasp, tryin' to get her attention.

When she finally turns to see what I want, Mrs. Morgan lets out a gasp: "Jack."

Everything turns to dead silence. He must've heard everything Mama was sayin' about him. He just stands there with his hands in his pockets, then in a low voice says, "Danny said I'd find you here, Stella. Can I talk to you, alone?"

Stella looks at Mama, then slowly gets up, and walks away with him. I'm sittin' here waitin' for my mama to attack him, and she just sits there. *What is goin' on here? Isn't this the man we were just gonna feed to the lions?*

"Mama," I yell, "aren't you gonna stop him?"

Mama is rearranging herself on her lounge chair, still pretty ruffled that Mr. Morgan surprised us like that. "A. J., as much as I'd like to help Mrs. Morgan, I can't fight this battle for her. I've told Mrs. Morgan what I think, but when it comes down to it, she's the one who has to live with her decisions. I'll tell you one thing ..." Mama looks around to make sure no one is listenin' to her this time ... "it's a whole lot easier for a woman to keep a good man good than it is to try and turn a jerk into a prince."

"You mean 'turn a frog into a prince,' don't you, Mama—like in the fairy tales?"

"You're right, excuse my French. Let's just say, the best you can shoot for, kiddo, is to find yourself a prince from the get-go."

"Was Daddy a prince from the get-go, Mama?"

"Indeed he was."

"How did you know that he was a prince?"

Mama chomps on few potato chips while she's thinkin'. "Well ... for one thing, he had the example of his own father, who taught him to be respectful of women. And for another, your father was the only man alive whose head didn't snap out of joint whenever *Christelle Clarion* strutted by. When he was with me, he never gave another woman the time of day. Those are a few good signs of a prince."

"Who's Christelle Clarion?" I could tell by the way Mama said her name, she was somethin', but *what kind of somethin'*?

"Christelle," Mama said, as she thrust her nose in the air, like she was acting her out, "was a little French doll who had all the boys tripping over themselves every time she walked by. She also had her eye on the hunk of Squawkomish High, namely, *Sonny Degulio*, but don't you ever tell him I admitted that to you. Anyway, Miss Clarion's only goal in life was to snatch him away from me."

"But Daddy always says *you* were the most beautiful girl in high school."

"Well, let's just say Christelle gave me a run for the money when she decided she wanted my man."

"So why didn't Daddy look at her when she was all dolled up?"

Mama lifts her sun hat off her head like she's lifting off the years since her high school days. "I asked him that once." She looks out over the water like she's hearin' him say it all again. "'Why would I want to look at a ruby, when I'm already holding a diamond?' That's what he said. Then he told me I was the one he wanted to marry someday."

"Really? Did he say he'd rather marry an Italian glamour queen, instead of a French doll? Is *that* what he said?"

"Well, not *exactly.* This part I remember word for word. He said, 'The day I laid eyes on you, Sophia Gulliano, I knew these eyes would never be satisfied looking at any woman but you for the rest of my life. So marry me, or leave me a ruined man.'"

"Wow. That is *so romantic.* What'd you say back, Mama?"

"Oh, something eloquent, like, 'Is *that so?'"*

"That's all you said, after he said *all that?"*

Mama chomps on a few more chips, tryin' to remember. "Oh, yep, I did say something more. I said, 'May the good Lord strike you blind if you don't live up to those fancy words of yours, Sonny Degulio.' That's why he always looks nervous and throws his hands over his eyes whenever a pretty woman walks by."

"Oh, *that's* why he does that. But he's not blind yet, is he, Mama?"

"No, he is not." Mama smiles.

"But, how will I know when I find my prince?"

Mama looks at me real good. "A. J., if there is one thing you got from your mama, it's a strong head to go after what you want in life. I don't expect you'll settle for anything less than a prince."

That reminds me that Danny's havin' to see his daddy again, and I have a strong hunch where I can find him. Me and Sailor show up on Juniper Beach and, sure enough, there's Danny standin' at the shore, right where we found him last time he was thinkin' about his daddy.

"Hey," he says when he sees us.

"So, your daddy's here, huh?"

"Yeah. He's here."

"Talked to him yet?" I ask.

"Nope. Just enough to tell him where to find my mama."

"You think he'll talk her into goin' home?"

"Can't say. But she'll be crazy if she goes." Danny starts throwin' rocks into the water, just like last time.

"Maybe he came to say he's sorry." I'm tryin' to think of something good here to say.

"Well, if he is, it's only because he's gettin' hungry and there's no one around to cook for him. Won't be any different once he gets her back. Just like before."

I can tell I'm just makin' him madder, because the more I talk, the harder he's throwin' those rocks.

"Well, we're gonna go now." We start to walk away, but I just have to tell him one more thing. "Maybe God will help your daddy to change."

Danny looks up and shrugs. "Maybe."

He doesn't look like he believes me, but I don't tell him that I lit a candle at church for his daddy. Whenever you do that, I think God knows you mean business.

Me and Sailor are on our way back through the woods and stop by the cemetery to visit my dead animals. I'm startin' to wonder what they look like by now, after they've been buried for so long, but I don't really want to know. So I try and picture what they will look like if God brings them back to life in heaven. I'm just gettin' this heavenly scene of me in my little white robe, leading all my animals around the garden of Eden, when I hear someone comin' through the woods. Sailor's hair stands up, and he starts barkin'. That makes me scared, 'cause Sailor hardly ever barks at people. I stand up and get ready to run for home, when I realize it's Jack. For some reason I can't think of him as Mr. Morgan, only Jack. I think it's because when I say Mr. or Mrs., I think of nice family people.

He sees us standin' there and comes over to us. "Hey," he says. "You're the Degulio girl, aren't you?"

"Yes, sir," I answer. He looks like the kind of man I should be scared of, but I don't feel scared anymore for some reason.

"I'm lookin' for my son Danny. Have you seen him?" he asks.

"Just seen him at the beach," I say.

“The beach down this way?” he says, pointin’ down the trail toward Juniper Beach.

“Yes, sir, but … I’m not sure you want to go there right now.”

“Why’s that?” he asks, lookin’ at me funny.

“Well, if you’re askin’ me, I don’t think Danny feels much like talkin’ right now, sir. If you try and talk to him, he’ll probably just start throwin’ a bunch of rocks into the water.”

“Throwin’ rocks? What are you talkin’ about, throwin’ rocks?” He’s lookin’ awfully confused.

“Well … that’s what he does every time I start to talk about you, throws rocks into the water.”

“Tell you what,” he says to me. “How ’bout you call me Jack instead of sir, and tell me what your name is, and maybe we can talk like friends about why Danny doesn’t want to talk to me.”

“Umm, okay … Jack.” Now I feel funny callin’ him that out loud. He’s the only grown-up I know tellin’ me to call them by their first name—well, besides Buzz, but that’s different; he’s always been just Buzz. “My name is A. J., and this is Sailor, and it might take awhile to tell you why Danny doesn’t want to talk to you.”

“Well, A. J., I have all the time in the world, if you would be kind enough to fill me in.” Then he sits right down on a log and waits for me to start talkin’.

I figure I may as well sit down too or my legs might wear out just standin’ in one place. “Well, you see, si—uh, Jack, when you had that sleepover at your house with that other lady … well, that just broke Mrs. Morgan’s heart. My mama said that would be like tearin' a woman's heart in so many pieces it would take forever to put it back together. And I thought of it more like when my Grandma Angelina had her pet cow shot. See, Elsie trusted them with all her heart, and then one day, *pow*. They shot her dead. Broke the trust, big-time.

"Danny loves his mama, and when you do somethin' like that to his mama, well, he's not goin' to be very happy with you. Besides, he says it's happened before, and he thinks it will happen again if his mama goes back to you. That's why he throws rocks whenever I talk about you.... Know what I mean?"

Jack sits there real still for a long time, then says, "Well, A. J., thank you for lettin' me in on that." He looks pretty sad, and I feel kind of bad for him.

I look over at him and say, "I lit a candle for you at church Sunday and asked God to help you change. He can help you if you ask Him."

"A. J.," he says, "you are probably the only person in the whole world who isn't afraid to tell me to my face what a fool I am." Then he gets up and walks down the pitchy pine trail that leads neither to the beach nor to Big Chief. I walk back to the cabin wondering, *When did I ever call him a fool?*

When I get home, I open the back door and find Mrs. Morgan sittin' with my mama. Mrs. Morgan is cryin'. There sure is a lot of hurt goin' 'round on this island right now. Mama looks at me like I'd better go back outside. I see Adriana's shadow through the front curtain.

She's sittin' on the porch swing, so I go out the front door to see her, but then I see she isn't alone. Jason is sittin' next to her. I didn't realize until now that he'd returned with his dad. Now I'm just standin' here feelin' stupid.

Nothin' feels quite right anymore around here. I wish these Morgans would just all go away so we could have our island back. They have been nothin' but trouble since they got here. Except for Danny. He saved my life, so he can stay if he wants to.

After everyone has gone home, Mama comes to say good night to me. She tells me that Mrs. Morgan has decided to stay on the island and will not be going back with Mr. Morgan for now. That makes me feel a little relieved for Danny. I don't tell my mama about my talk with Jack. I don't know if I would be in trouble for that or not, but I don't want to find out. After she turns out my light, I lie here in the dark thinkin' about everything. In a weird way, I feel kinda sorry for Jack. I don't know why I would ever feel sorry for a man like that, but I've never seen a grown man look so sad.

Danny hung around on our dock after him and J. R. got back from their morning fishin' trip. I don't think he wants to spend much time at Big Chief anymore. Adriana's happier than I've seen her all month and is walkin' down the beach with Jason when Danny sees them. I can tell it bothers Danny to see them together.

"Does Jason still have his other girlfriend?" I ask him.

"'Fraid so," he says. "Matter of fact, Jason told me last

night that he gave his girl back home a St. Christopher, and they're supposedly going steady now."

J. R. cuts in and says, "Can anyone talk about anything around this place besides heartbreakin' men and cryin' women? For Pete's sake, I feel like I'm living in a soap opera."

"You're right, let's go dive for bottles," Danny says.

For once they let me come along. They must figure we can all use a break from the whole mess.

After dinner, we all start up a game of cards—everyone but Adriana, who's obviously on another "walk." Danny's still here and doesn't seem like he's plannin' to leave anytime soon.

Mama and Daddy quit playin' after one round of rummy, and they are readin' their books on the couch next to us. For once things feel back to normal, the way it felt before the Morgans came.

Halfway through the next game, Adriana comes through the door glowing from ear to ear, lookin' like she's just won the Miss America contest. We all look at her waitin' for the reason behind her moment of glory. "Guess what?" she says and holds up some shiny thing hangin' around her neck. "Jason just gave me a St. Christopher. We're going steady."

18

Crosswinds

It has been three days since Adriana gave us the "bad news." Danny asked Jason what in the world he thought he was doin' when he was already goin' steady with a girl back home. Jason told him there was nothing wrong with havin' two girlfriends; after all, he wasn't married.

This just makes me so sad for Adriana. In her mind she is married, no matter what Jason says. I know if I tell her about the other girlfriend, she won't believe me and will just tell me to stay out of her business. Then if Jason lies about it, she'll really want to kill me. But someone has to tell her—someone she'll listen to.

I feel like Mama and Daddy need to know about this, and maybe she'll listen to them. Daddy won't let anyone hurt her like that if he knows about it. He might even tell Island Boy to take back his St. Christopher and get lost. But then Adriana will hate me even more. Maybe she doesn't have to know I'm the one that told them.

It's pourin' down rain outside, and the wind is blowin' like crazy. I can't sleep anyway thinkin' about Adriana, so I go to Mama and Daddy's room and knock on the door. They're still up readin' with their light on, so I go in and sit on the end of their bed.

"What's up?" Daddy says.

"It's about Adriana, Daddy. I'm worried about her."

"You, worried about your sister? This must be pretty serious," he jokes.

"Yeah. It is. Danny told me that Jason already has another girlfriend back in Oklahoma and is going steady with her, too. Danny told him that was wrong, and he said he could have two girlfriends at the same time if he wanted to because he isn't married. But Adriana would feel really bad if she knew, and it just isn't right."

Mama and Daddy look at each other, and they aren't smilin' anymore. "That family just doesn't learn, do they?" Mama says to Daddy.

Just then the door opens wide, and Adriana steps inside. "Talking about me, are you, A. J? I know you were talking about me and Jason, I heard our names, so don't try and deny it."

"It's not what you think, Adriana; it's somethin' else. I was worried about you. I'm tryin' to help you...."

Adriana looks at me like she doesn't believe a word I'm sayin'. I know she thinks I'm telling on her and Jason for kissin' in my critter cemetery.

"Well, A. J., I'm *worried* about you, too," she says in a mean voice. "I'm worried that you're going to grow up with a stupid animal obsession if I don't help you. I can ruin your little secret just like you had to ruin my birthday by crying your head off over that bonehead dog of yours.

"Well, I wonder what mom and dad would do if they knew about your stinky little secret out in the shed. Would they finally put an end to this crazy animal problem of yours, or let you just keep it, and baby you like they always do? And if they don't do anything, I will. I'll go turn that red-eyed vampire rat loose tonight, and she can just die out there in the storm for all I care."

I look at Mama and Daddy, and now they are lookin' at me to see if this is really true. I can't believe Adriana would do this to me. How could she tell them about Ruby? How *could* she? "I was just trying to *help* you," I cry and run from the room.

I rush out to the shed in the pourin' rain and grab Ruby's cage. Where can I go to save her? There is no way Mama and Daddy will let me keep Ruby after what Adriana just told them, and even if they do, Adriana will turn her loose to die anyway.

The only way to save Ruby is to get her off this island. And the only way off this island is by boat. I run down to the dock and untie the dinghy. Sailor is right behind me and jumps in with me. I don't even care that it's pitch dark and the wind is blowin' rain in my face. All I can think about is saving Ruby.

I jab the oars into the oarlocks and start to row. No one can see me from the cabin, so if I can just get away before they realize the boat is missing I should be able to save her. All I have to do is get to the mainland. If I can hide the cage somewhere by the gas dock, then row back to the island, I can call Dorie in the morning and tell her where I hid the cage, and her mom can drive her out to get Ruby. It has to work—it just has to.

I'm rowing downlake toward the gas dock, but there's a crosswind blowin' me toward the shore. The only thing on the mainland before you reach the gas dock is Pirate's Cove, where all the rocks jet out into the water, and there's no way to get to shore with a boat.

It's just so dark out I can't see how much farther I have to go before I need to turn toward shore. But the wind is pushin' us that direction so hard that the dinghy is goin' toward shore no matter how hard I try to row straight.

I have Ruby's cage covered with my jacket to keep her dry, but I am freezin' cold. My arms are tired, and my hands are numb. I feel just like I did when I drifted downlake and Danny had to rescue me. If only he would come now and take Ruby to shore for me.

I can barely even row anymore. The wind is just too strong. All I can do is drift to shore and pray we've already passed Pirate's Cove.

Just as I'm thinkin' that, the dinghy bashes into something, and Ruby's cage slides off the seat to the floor. It's so dark and rainy, I can't even see. The waves keep smashing us harder and harder into the rocks. *Pirate's Cove.* I feel water pouring in all around me. I can't see. I can't see. "Sailor," I'm cryin' and clinging to him for dear life. The water—it's all around me. I no longer feel the boat beneath me. *Ruby ... where's Ruby ... Jesus, where's Jesus ...*

I'm holdin' Sailor's collar, that's all I feel, and the water's covering my face. He's swimming, and I'm holdin' on … my head—it hurts … it hurts.…

I'm dreaming, but I can't wake up. I feel sunlight on my face, but I can't open my eyes. I hear voices, I hear my name, but I can't answer.

I'm in a warm place with softness all around me. I hear Mama's voice, and she's cryin'. She's holdin' my hand and sayin', "Come back, A. J., please come back."

I'm tryin' to open my eyes. I push and push, and they barely open. I see Mama, and she screams, "She's back. Sonny, she's back." Then I see Daddy, then all of my brothers, then Adriana … Adriana is crying. Then I remember.

Sailor. "Where's Sailor?" I whisper.

"Right here, A. J.," Daddy says, and Sailor comes over and licks my face, and I start to cry.

"I was in the water, I hit my head.… Sailor … was there.…" I feel my head where it hit the rocks. Bandages are wound all around my head like a turban.

"Sailor must have … brought you to shore," Daddy chokes up.

"… Ruby … my Ruby …?" I feel hot tears roll down my face. "My Ruby drown?"

"I'm so sorry, A. J. …" Adriana sobs.

I couldn't look at her.

"Who found me, Daddy? Whose voice did I hear when I couldn't wake up?"

"Jack found you, A. J. He was out looking all night

for you with the rest of us. He found you at Pirate's Cove at daybreak—with Sailor by your side. "

Jack found me. I close my eyes. "I'm so tired."

"You sleep now," Mama whispers and strokes my forehead, like when I'm sick and have a fever.

I wake a long while later to my daddy's voice. "A. J., someone's here who'd like to see you."

I open my eyes. Jack's standin' in my doorway.

"Jack," I whisper.

"I'll let you two talk a bit," Daddy says and closes the door.

Jack walks over to the bed real slow. I look up at him and try to smile, even though it hurts. "Thanks for findin' me," I say.

He looks down at me real tender like, and for a moment I swear I see Danny in his eyes.

"It's me who needs to thank you, A. J. I may have found you, but because of you, I think Jesus found me again."

"He did?" I ask, surprised.

"When I found you, A. J., I thought you were gone. You lay there still as a rock, and all I could do while I was lookin' down at you was think of every word you said to me the other day. And I remembered what you said about how you lit that candle for me and asked God to change me. Well, I kneeled down over you, and I prayed that if God could change a man, would He start with me?" Then he starts to cry.

"When I looked at you, A. J., I saw myself as a little boy at my grandma's old church, kneelin' down at the altar and askin' Jesus to be my Savior, and then I realized, I had known Him once before. But it has been a long time since I last asked Him for anything."

"You thought I was dead?" I ask him. I always wondered what it would be like to have someone think you were dead—just like in *Tom Sawyer.*

"When you started to move, A. J., it was like God was givin' back your life and my life all at the same time. I know I've hurt a lot of people, but I'm askin' God to help me change. You really think He can change a man like me?"

"Sure He can. Just look at St. Paul. He went around killin' all the Christians before God told him to knock it off. He even let Paul become a Christian himself. You're not much worse than him."

I've had to spend three long days in bed to make sure my head's gonna be all right. They think I might get dizzy and fall if I get up too soon. I'm just glad I'm in my own bed with Sailor by my side. I don't remember ever bein' in the hospital, but I guess I was until Dr. Starky got me released by agreeing to treat me on the island. They said I was thrashin' all around and yellin' that I wanted to go home, so Mama begged him to get me out of there. Once I got here, I passed out for two days.

Dr. Starky's here to check up on my stitches. He says I took quite a head bashing at Pirate's Cove. According to Dr. Starky, most kids only take thirty stitches, but it took forty to hold my brain in 'cause it's so big.

Daddy starts sayin' that the reason they got me released so fast from the hospital was 'cause I was screamin' so loud about goin' home that kids in the other rooms started rumors about me bein' a lost Martian who was being held captive. "Then when they wheeled you out with that big cone on your head, everyone believed it."

"Daddy, you're makin' that up, aren't you?"

Daddy and Dr. Starky keep tellin' jokes while he's checkin' my stitches. They finally have to stop 'cause it hurts every time I start to laugh.

I'm pretty sure that Dr. Starky doesn't remember Daddy as bein' the nut on the bow of the pink boat. But when he goes to leave, he says, "Oh, by the way, Sonny, that is one fine seacraft you have there. Let me know if you ever decide to part with it."

Everyone has been so nice to me, I wish I could get this kind of treatment without havin' to bash my head on a rock. Even Adriana has been nice. She comes in to see if I want ice cream or something to drink, or she brings me new comic books to read. It's still hard for me to see her though; it always reminds me of Ruby. Matter of fact, Adriana is standin' at my door again right now.

"Hey, can I come in?"

"Yeah." *I guess I have nothing better to do.*

She comes and sits on the end of my bed. The first thing I look for is that stupid St. Christopher that started this whole thing. They say he's the protector of children. Well, if it were up to me, I think they should desaint him at the Vatican for not doin' his job.

Not only did he *not* protect me from smashin' my head on the rocks, but what kind of saint would allow an innocent hamster to drown? Besides, he's the reason I told my parents about Adriana in the first place. If he hadn't been hangin' around her neck like some trophy, I would never have gotten myself into this mess.

"Where's your Christopher?" I ask. I will no longer address him as Saint.

Adriana looks down at the place he once hung. "I gave it back," she says.

"You … gave … you *broke up* with Jason?" I'm shocked.

"No boy is more important than my own sister, A. J., especially one who's a disloyal two-timer."

"Wow. What did he say when you gave it back?" *This will be a great twist for my diary.*

"He was all defensive at first, but after he found out what happened to you, he realized that he was hurting a lot of people. Jack had a talk with him and told him they didn't need more than one fool in their family, and that he already filled that position himself."

"I don't think Jack is a fool anymore, do you, Adriana?"

"I'd say between you and Jesus, Jack doesn't have a fighting chance to stay a fool. You two are the only thing he talks about anymore, how Jesus brought you into his life, so you could bring his life back to Jesus. Even Mom is starting to believe there's something different about that man."

"What about Danny and his mama? Do they believe it?"

"I think they are just watching him for a while, trying to figure out if this is real or not. It's hard when you've been hurt before."

"Well, I believe it. I could see it in his eyes when he came to see me. When someone has Jesus in their soul, you can see it in their eyes. You know why, Adriana?"

"No, A. J., why?" This time she looks at me like she really cares what I have to say.

"Because when you have the Light of the World living inside of your soul, He shines out of you anywhere He can."

19

Grace

Today is a special day in history for this island, especially for Juniper Beach. There is a new sign hangin' on a tree there in honor of Jack Morgan. Ever since Jack found Jesus again, he has insisted on gettin' baptized right here in the same lake that I nearly drowned in.

The Baptist preacher is on vacation for two weeks, so we went to our church to talk to the priest about helping Jack get baptized. The priest said he'd be happy to help, as long as Jack went through their baptism classes and got baptized in their holy fountain.

Jack said that the lake is where God gave him his life back, and he refuses to get sprinkled with some holy water in a cement tub. Jesus never did it that way Himself, he told the priest, and this lake water is every bit as holy as their water because the same Hand that made this water made theirs. He also told him he didn't need classes because he has read about it in the Bible, and it's not all that complicated.

The priest wouldn't go for it, so we went to the Baptist youth pastor who said he'd be honored to baptize Jack on Juniper Beach. I gotta hand it to the Baptists on that one. They act so excited to baptize anyone, anywhere, that must be how they got their name.

It is a warm summer morning, and there's a lot of people on Juniper Beach. I almost hated to give away the secret, but when I showed this beach to Jack, he fell in love with it. He promised that if I shared my secret beach, he would hang a sign that was sure to keep the majority of Squawkomish from coming on its shores.

TRESPASSERS WILL BE BAPTIZED

He said that way, if anyone does come ashore, we'll know we've got a good reason to welcome them.

Everyone from our family and Jack's family, as well as half of the Baptist church, has showed up for this event. The good thing about that is, those Baptists are into this whole potluck thing, and there is more food piled on these tables than I could eat in a month.

Everyone's gathered at the shoreline, and Jack walks into the water with the pastor. I'm already choked up at this point, just watchin' Jack. He's lookin' so serious, as if he's walkin' right toward the cross at Calvary. The pastor asks Jack if he has put his trust in the Lord Jesus Christ. He says, yes, he has. Then the pastor says, "On your profession of faith in the Lord Jesus Christ, I baptize you, Jack Morgan, in the name of the Father, the

Son, and the Holy Spirit," and under the water he goes.

When he comes up, everyone is cryin'. It's like seein' a man who was dead go under, and a man who's alive come out. He gets to that shore, and the first person there huggin' his daddy and weepin' is Danny. And next to Danny is his mama.

When Jack sees his wife standin' there in front of him, he reaches out and touches her small face with his big rough hand, like he is touchin' a precious jewel. He's drippin' wet, but you can still see the tears fallin' from his face. Jason comes over after that and hugs his daddy too.

I am standin' here lookin' at this family who was all in pieces and is now together, and nobody can tell me that there ain't no God.

By the time all the Baptists have left the island, we have so much food left over, Mama suggests we have a farewell feast for the Morgan family later this evenin'. She figures it will take a few hours before anyone will be hungry enough to eat again. She even suggests we have it right on Juniper Beach at sunset.

Mama thinks it would be fun to surprise the Morgans, so we spend the entire afternoon fixin' up Juniper Beach to look like a fancy lakeside restaurant.

Mama goes to town, haulin' out all the tiki torches and chinese lanterns from The Big Island Bash to light up the place after the sun goes down.

Daddy sets up two long tables, pushed together to look like one, that Adriana covers with white bedsheets. They look just like fancy white tablecloths once she sets some candles and fresh flowers in the middle. We hang the chinese lanterns from overhanging tree boughs at the entrance to the beach and stake the tiki torches around the table.

J. R. is busy buildin' the campfire for after-dinner marshmallows and a few fireworks that Daddy "confiscated" from some state park campers, because they were a fire hazard.

Daddy hands the stash of starburst cones to J. R. and says, "Son, I'm assigning you the responsibility of destroying these potentially hazardous pyrotechnics somewhere around ten o'clock tonight, as a service to the Idaho Department of Parks and Recreation."

J. R. loves it when Daddy does things like that. I think Daddy figures that, if we do happen to start a fire here on the island, there will be a very limited number of bodies to recover, compared to burnin' down the entire state park.

I get to be in charge of paintin' a fancy name on a big slab of driftwood to hang at the entrance of our lakeside bistro. While it's dryin' in the sun, Mama makes me lie down and rest my head awhile back at the cabin. She and Adriana come back while I'm sleepin' to reassess all the leftovers we'd brought back earlier. Once they finish arranging everything on pretty serving platters, the three of us carry it all back to Juniper Beach.

While we're walkin' toward the beach, Adriana says, "Oh, by the way, A. J., Daddy invited the Gizmodes to join us for dinner tonight. Little Rodney stopped by the cabin to see you, but I told him you were sleeping and would see him at dinner."

"What? Are you serious?"

"Dead serious. He's been really worried about you. He asked if he could sit by you tonight, and even brought you some daisies."

"No dang way." My head's startin' to hurt just thinkin' about it. "C'mon, Adriana, you gotta get me outta this. I'll stay at the cabin. Tell him I have a headache, anything...."

"Honestly, A. J., just because he wears high-water jeans with red cowboy boots is no reason to hide from the poor guy. I think his matching red cowboy hat looks kind of cool, really."

When I look at Adriana, I see her mouth startin' to twitch. "You're a big fat liar."

Adriana's laughin' so hard she's doubled over her bowl of potato salad.

"You think that's funny?" Then I start laughin' out of pure relief that it's not true. "When I see Rodney at catechism, I'll have him tell his big brother that you're ready for that big slobbery Hawaiian kiss he's been savin' up for you."

When Adriana finally comes up for air, she says, "*Yuck*. I'd rather kiss a baboon."

It feels good to laugh with my sister again.

Mama takes a good look around, eyeballin' every little detail, until not a thing is left undone or out of place, then sends me to go round up the Morgans. "And don't spill the beans about the Juniper Beach Lakeshore Dining Establishment and Bistro."

"Don't worry, Mama, I couldn't repeat all that if I tried."

I return a short time later with the Morgans in tow. I'm tryin' to see all of this through their eyes, as if I wasn't expectin' anything. It looks so great, it even surprises me. Mama has the twins at the entrance to greet us. In their white shirts and little black bow ties they look like midget maître d's. There is no way on earth they would ever agree to wear those little bows unless Mama made them.

The Morgans just stand in awe with their mouths hangin' open like they can't believe what we've done.

Jack says, "I must have drowned when I was gettin' baptized, and this must be heaven."

Mrs. Morgan looks at my mama and smiles. "Who but you, Sophia?"

The only one lookin' a little uncomfortable is Adriana, but she is doin' her best not to let it show. She hasn't spoken to Jason since the Christopher disaster.

Danny is still takin' in this whole restaurant scene. Finally he turns and looks at me. "Wow."

I just smile and nod.

The sun is just settin' when we all sit down together. Jack offers to say the blessing. I have never heard a man sound so thankful for everything in all my life. This is not "Bless us, O Lord, with these, Thy gifts." No one even cares that the food's gettin' cold. We are in the middle of somethin' good here.

Leftovers sure taste great when they're cooked by the Baptists. They have it down when it comes to fried chicken and Jell-O. I never knew there were so many varieties of

Jell-O salad in this world, and somehow they all ended up on our table. Sailor reminds me that he's lyin' under the table at my feet and hasn't gotten anything yet. *Sorry, boy, fat chance with this kind of cookin'.*

Everyone seems to be havin' a good time, includin' Adriana. Apart from avoiding eye contact with Jason, she's bein' unusually friendly to everyone. In between the fried chicken feast and dessert, Daddy surprises us all with an old Magnavox record player that he found at the cabin. He cranks up the handle, and an old scratchy song starts playin' away. It's great to have real dinner music at our outdoor restaurant.

For dessert, Mama's servin' up hot coffee from a thermos to the grown-ups, and devil's food cake with fluffy white frostin'. Why on earth they call something that good "devil's food" I will never understand. Does that mean I have to confess it if I eat it?

While the grown-ups are all sippin' away and listenin' to music at one end of the table, us kids pull out a deck of cards and play Baloney at the other end. After the first round, Jason, who's been fidgety the whole game, looks at me and says, "Can I talk to you for a minute, A. J?"

"Umm, I guess so." *What would he want to talk to me for?*

"How about over by the campfire?" he says.

"Okay ..." I get up and head toward the fire. Sailor follows at my heels. I shoot Adriana a *what's this about?* look. She just shrugs her shoulders like she doesn't have a clue. Danny urges me on with his eyes like it's gonna be okay. Maybe he knows what's up.

As soon as we're out of earshot from everyone, Jason turns to me and says, "Look, A. J., I just need you to know that what happened to you ..." Then he looks down and can't finish what he's tryin' to say. He looks away for a minute, then whispers, "I'm really sorry."

Now my eyes start to water up, and I'm not sure why. All I can do is nod my head. I look back at the table. "I'm okay," I say. "I'm not so sure about Adriana."

Jason glances over there too. "Yeah, I know. She may not feel like talkin' to a jerk right now, but would you ask her if she'll come talk to me anyway?"

I walk back over to Adriana and tell her that Jason wants to talk to her. She looks at me like she's not so sure she wants to go, but she gets up and goes over there anyway. I just stand here starin' at the lake and feel like ten pounds just lifted from my head. I don't hate Jason anymore. I look back and see him talkin' to Adriana. Maybe there's hope for Island Boy after all. Maybe there's hope for all of us.

When I got hurt, it looked like it only happened to me, but it happened to everyone. And when Jack hurt Mrs. Morgan, it hurt everyone. My sins hurt a lot of people too, including a hamster. It's just like Sister Abigail says, "There's no such thing as secret sins."

The sun has just gone down on Juniper Beach. The grown-ups are still chattin' away over coffee, with sweet scratchy music playin' in the background. Jason and Adriana are still talkin' by the fire. Danny points out the Bear constellation to me and laughs when I tell him my head might fall off if I tip it back too far to look up. He sounds just like Little Joe Cartwright when he laughs.

Bright paper lanterns and tiki torches flicker around our card game, as a burst of sparks explode overhead and shower down around us. This is just the way I want to remember our last night with the Morgans.

Monday mornin' the Morgan family is busy packin' up to head back to Oklahoma. I am so sad that they are leavin' I can hardly stand the thought of this island without them. *They finally get put back together, and then they leave us. What kind of deal is that?*

Mama says we could probably fill the entire lake twice over with all the tears she has seen here this summer. Says she has never seen so many different kinds of tears in all her life. Tears of heartache, tears of remorse, tears of fear, tears of gratefulness, tears of forgiveness, and tears of joy. She also says it may take awhile for all of those hearts to heal up, but the Morgans are returnin' home as a family, and that's what matters most.

They promise us they'll try and come back next summer to see us. Whether they come back or not, one thing I know, I will never forget this summer for as long as I live.

I'm headin' over to Big Chief with some banana muffins that I made the Morgans for their trip home. I put in a little too much bakin' powder, so Daddy calls them "sky-high" muffins. He told me to duck when I went through the door so I wouldn't scrape the tops off of them.

I look a little silly still walkin' around with this big turban on my head, but that's the price you have to pay for holdin' your brain in your head, I guess. I feel like Little Red Riding Hood going through the woods with my basket of sky-highs and this big cone on my head. Sailor's here to protect me from the big bad wolves, if any are lurking out here.

When I get to Big Chief, I can't bring myself to knock on the door. These are the kind of people that you just can't say good-bye to. I leave my basket on the front porch and head back toward Papoose. I'll just have to wait for them to come say good-bye to us.

I make my way down to the dock and dangle my feet over the end. I'm lookin' at my reflection next to Sailor's in the water. I remember back to the day I saved Sailor. Then I remember the night Sailor saved me. This much I know for sure, a big God has watched over us.

Daddy comes down to the dock sayin' that Grandma Juliana just called from Italy. She says one of her relatives has just passed away and left a hilltop villa to her. She insists we all go live in Tuscany with her so we'll be there to bury her when she dies in her homeland.

Daddy says she's too stubborn to ever die, but if we don't go, we'll have to listen to her whine about it, long-distance-collect, for the rest of our lives.

Mama, of course, who is always up for somethin' new, thinks this is the opportunity of a lifetime and is certain it will be a great adventure for us all.

Me, I'm willin' to go wherever the wind wants to take me. That might sound kind of funny after seein' where the winds have taken me this summer. But it's not the wind I've come to trust. I trust in the One who sends the wind.

Epilogue (For all you hopeless romantics out there)

In the fall of 1968, my family moved to Tuscany. My one regret was having to leave Sailor behind. My sole comfort was that Danny agreed to keep him for me until I could return one day.

We wrote letters frequently on behalf of Sailor. Every once in a while we would remember to mention his name.

My family loved Italy, especially my mother, who opened a posh little guest hotel, Sophia's Villa di Ritz, which has kept her in her element, catering to rich American tourists. No surprise to anyone, Grandma Juliana is still alive and … well, let's just say she's still alive. She resides with all of her statues at her Villa di Dolce Far Niente, translated, "Palace of Sweet Inactivity," where a loving staff is paid a fortune to care for her—and her … *eccentric* behavior.

Adriana was swept up as a runway model and bought a small flat in Milan. She quickly became savvy to European men and refers to most of them as arrogant *nudniks*,

Yiddish for "talkative bores." She says the two most useful words in the Italian language have been, *"Ciao, bambino."* The only guy in her life right now is Pip, her toy poodle.

In the winter of 1975, Danny's grandfather passed away and left the island to his favorite grandson. Danny became the youth pastor at the Squawkomish Baptist Church.

On my eighteenth birthday, I left Italy and flew back to the States to begin my college courses in veterinary medicine. First stop, Indian Island—to see Sailor, of course ...

Drifting Again

Indian Lake, Idaho
July 1976

Stepping onto the dock is like stepping back in time. Nestled among the overgrowth is little Papoose, a lost cabin waiting for its family to return. Voices and laughter still echo from its walls: Mama, Daddy, Adriana, J. R., Dino, and Benji.

I sneak inside feeling very smug that I still have the key, and no one else on earth knows that I'm here. The number to Big Chief is taped to the wall by the phone. I pick up the receiver and begin to dial. My hands begin to shake. I pray I can pull this off....

Three rings ...

"Hello?"

That same Southern voice that made my heart pound the first time I heard it is making it pound again now.

"Well, howdy on ya," I bellow, in the best darn Southern drawl I can muster. My Southern language has slowly been replaced with Italian over the past eight years.

There's a long pause. "May I ask who's callin'?" the voice says.

"Well … you can ask all ya want to, but I ain't gonna tell ya."

"Who *is this?"*

"Don't you recognize a true Southern belle when you hear one, Danny Boy?"

That definitely gets the wheels turning.

"A. J.? … Is that you?"

"Bingo. Race you to Juniper Beach," I yell. "And bring my dog." Then I slam down the phone and dart out the screen door so fast it nearly flies off its hinges.

The first thing I see when I reach Juniper Beach is my big *old* dog. "Sailor," I cry. Tears start streaming down my face. He comes barreling down the beach and pounces on me so hard I nearly fall over. I bury my face in his fur and sob like I did the day I found him on death row. Then I see Danny—but this is not the Danny I remember.

When we're within about five feet of each other, we come to a complete standstill. Eight years is a long time when you've gone from saying good-bye as children to saying hello as adults.

"Hey, A. J.," he says, real tender.

No one has *ever* said my name the way Danny says my name. I'm staring at a man with the build of The Duke and the cutes of Little Joe Cartwright, and I find myself wanting to ask if he can ride a horse.

The sky is full of stars, and the moon is so bright it reflects off the water like a river. It's a perfect night for a moonlit row. We climb into the old dinghy and shove out to sea.

"Which way, A. J.?" Danny asks me.

"Let's just drift."

So we lay the oars on the floorboards, and we're on our way....

Two drifters, off to see the world, there's such a lot of world to see. We're after the same rainbow's end, waitin' round the bend, my huckleberry friend, Sailor, and me....

Not necessarily the end ...

Author's Epilogue

Sometimes I will read a story that is so sad, I'm relieved to be able to tell myself it's not true. On the other hand, there have been stories that have touched me in such a way that I wish with all my heart they were true.

Although *Saving Sailor* is considered to be a work of fiction, you may find it fascinating to know that in 1968 there really was an Italian-American family of seven who spent their summers on a small island in the Northwest. They rented a pink boat they named the *African Queen*, dove for old bottles on a white sandy beach, hand-cranked fresh peach ice cream, and were blessed with an incredible sense of humor. Their magnum opus in life was finding joy and humor in whatever life dished up.

Coincidentally, there was a quirky young girl who loved animals to a fault, had an albino hamster hidden in her closet, released caught fish, rescued strays, buried the dead in hand-dug graves with stick crosses, and held little funerals. She also feared getting stuck in confessionals, drove her parents half crazy, and had a big hairy dog that meant the world to her. And when he went rowing with her, he really did wear a life jacket.

The promise I made to God out on the water that summer of 1968, I've kept to this day. I have not had a year since I would trade for that year. Life seemed simpler and sweeter then.

... And it really *doesn't* get any better than driftin' with your dog on a sunny afternoon, when you are young and your heart is full of dreams....

Author Interview

1. How did you start writing? What was your first piece of writing like?

I won a writing contest in second grade with my story "The Enchanted Princess." I remember getting to design the bulletin board with my story and characters, but I can't remember why the princess was enchanted.

When I finished college, I wasn't sure what I wanted to do, but I remembered I once loved to write so I joined a local writing group. I entered another writing contest and submitted a story about a dog that got hit by a car and was taken to the emergency animal hospital in the middle of the night by a cute young lady. The veterinarian saved the dog's life and also happened to be incredibly handsome. He and the cute lady fell in love. I titled it "Puppy Love." Needless to say, I didn't win that contest, but I did keep writing!

2. Why do you write fiction?

I am a born daydreamer and hopeless romantic. I also suffered from insomnia throughout my childhood. It's the perfect combination for becoming a fiction writer. I had a little soap opera going on in my head every night while waiting to fall asleep. Some nights I could hardly wait to go to bed to see what would happen next. I added to the story each night. Some of them went on for months, even years. By the time I grew up, I had volumes of stories to draw from.

I enjoy the freedom I find in writing fiction, the ability to go anywhere in the world, be any character, make anything happen, when I'm really just sitting in front of my computer. I'm very thankful for the gift of a good imagination. Nonfiction tends to be too limiting for me, whereas with fiction, the sky is the limit. I also love happy endings, which life can't always give us but fiction can.

3. Why do people remember a story more easily than a sermon?

I would say we remember a story better than a sermon because we can relate easier to a story. A sermon often suggests an ideal we should try and live up to. A story is the telling of an event in someone's life, and I for one love a story. Oftentimes in church I tend to drift in and out during a sermon, but the minute the pastor starts to use a personal story to make an application, I instantly tune back in. I still remember a story our pastor told about how he and his wife got in an argument on a trip to Victoria. When it came time for the boat to return to Seattle, neither one knew where the other was. One of them got on board; one didn't. I loved knowing that they were as idiotic as the rest of us. I don't have a clue what the sermon was, but I remember that story!

4. What do you hope readers will take away from your book?

I hope my readers will take many things away. First, I hope they will either remember or be drawn to a slower, simpler way of life. We seem to have lost the era of lazy summer days and replaced it with technology and hectic lifestyles. Drifting with a dog on a sunny afternoon has been replaced by hi-tech toys and hi-speed Internet. People and relationships are replaced with work and busyness. I hope *Saving Sailor* will help readers to recapture what's important in life.

I hope young people will be more cautious and prayerful about whom they entrust their hearts to. I hope they will seek for those people who will be trustworthy and true, and just as important, I hope they will be trustworthy and true themselves.

And I hope readers will come to know a big God who loves them, no matter what. Like A. J., if they seek Him, they will find Him.

5. Which character in the book is most like you?

A. J. reminds me of who I was as a child, curious, seeking, intense, quirky. A. J. has a heart for adventure, romance, and a desire to figure out the mysteries of life. Like A. J., I drove my family crazy with my intensity in trying to figure it all out. I drove my mom crazy by intentionally talking with a lisp and walking pigeon toed. The neighbor girl did both, and I thought it was cute.

When I went to summer camp, like A. J., I laid awake all night waiting for the Hatchet Man or Zodiac Killer to find me, depending on what spooky stories my cabinmates told after lights out. I remember waking up my camp counselors in the middle of the night and saying, "I can't sleep and feel like I'm losing my mind." Then I got to watch them try not to crack up laughing.

And, like A. J., I really did have a huge crush on Little Joe Cartwright.

6. What actor would you picture playing (your main character) in a movie?

Because I'm more of a reader than a moviegoer, I only know kid actors from the 1960s—when I was a kid. My favorite picks for playing A. J. would be a toss-up between Jodie Foster when she was ten years old, and Mary Badham who played Scout in *To Kill a Mockingbird*. They both had that zip and drive it would take to play A. J.

7. Which writers have influenced you most?

I loved Beverly Cleary and E. B. White. They wrote good, funny, wholesome stories with everything that makes a story good. As an adult I am still more drawn to children's books than adult books. I enjoy Kate DiCamillo for her ability to write stories that appeal to all ages and maintain wholesomeness and integrity. As far as adult novels, I think restrained and subtle affection is so much more romantic than explicit sex, and I appreciate writers who reflect those values in their writing. Some of the writers who have influenced me most as an adult did so because they wrote really well but their stories took a very dark turn halfway through. That's what spurred me on to write *Saving Sailor*. I was frustrated that such great stories had to turn so dark, so I decided to write my own story and conclude it the way I wished the other books had ended. I guess you could say I've been influenced by both good and bad writers.

8. Describe your writing process.

My writing process begins with a mix of true life events and what-ifs. I tend to write about topics I feel passionate about and put them into a fictional story. I've heard you should "write what you know," so when I set out to write a story, I often include as much true life material as necessary to make it credible and believable. Then I make up all of the what-ifs, fun characters, and favorable outcomes. I pretty much know how the story begins and ends, but I'm a firm believer in letting my characters write the story once we get going. That is the miraculous part of writing that I find so enjoyable and amazing; when you feel like you're just along for the ride, but your characters take on a life of their own.

A typical day of writing would begin with scoping out a place to write with my laptop. For instance, my favorite spot right now is sitting on my living room couch in front of my Christmas tree, watching the snow with Andy Williams Christmas music playing. I'm into atmosphere, but once I start writing, I'm gone to wherever my story takes place. I stay in that place until I'm yanked back out, usually by one of my kids yelling, "Mom, dinner's burning!" Then I remember I'm a mom, not my main character, and I have a family that is probably hungry. If I'm in a crucial spot in the story, I might sneak back later at night when everyone's in bed.

9. Can you share a particularly memorable encounter with a reader?

Some of my young readers invite me to teach writing workshops at their schools. When I tell the kids they will each have a story of their own by the end of the class, half of them look at me like I'm crazy. I put a fun visual of a desert island up on a screen in front of the classroom. The kids get to decide why they are there, how they got there, what happens to them during their stay, and how, or if, they ever get rescued. Without fail, the kids all come up with a great story, and most of them can't wait to read it to the class. One time a teacher came up to me after the workshop was over and said, "I just wanted to tell you that the little boy who just read his story is autistic. He's usually very withdrawn, and that is the first time he's *ever* volunteered to share something in front of the class. I've never seen him so excited about anything before."

I think everyone has a brilliant imagination somewhere inside of them just waiting to be sparked. I'm so amazed and honored when I see someone excited about writing.

10. What is one fact about yourself that readers might find most surprising?

I guess it might surprise people to know that I never thought of being a writer when I was growing up. Although I loved to write, I thought authors were a supernatural, predestined people group, like Santa Claus, The Beatles, Dr. Seuss, and The Tooth Fairy. I was planning to be a veterinarian with a farm full of stray animals. I did end up being an author with a farm full of stray animals, but no veterinarian degree.

Invite Renee Riva to Your Book Club

Transport your book club behind the scenes and into a new world by inviting Renee Riva to join in your group discussion via phone. To learn more, go to www.cookministries.com/readthis or e-mail Renee directly at reneeriva@gmail.com.

If your school or organization is interested in having Renee Riva for an author visit or writing workshop, please contact her Web site at www.reneeriva.com.

Also, visit www.cookministries.com/savingsailor to find a readers' guide for study questions and discussion to this book.